the LOVE EMERGENCY series

EMERGENCY
Engagement

the LOVE EMERGENCY series

EMERGENCY
Engagement

USA TODAY BESTSELLING AUTHOR
SAMANTHE BECK

Entangled Publishing
644 Shrewsbury Commons Ave
STE 181
Shrewsbury, PA 17361
rights@entangledpublishing.com

Brazen is an imprint of Entangled Publishing, LLC.

Edited by Heather Howland
Cover design by LJ Anderson/Mayhem Cover Creations
Cover art from Sara Eirew Photography

Manufactured in the United States of America

First Edition February 2016

**ENTANGLED
BRAZEN**

Dear Reader,

When I was a kid I broke my collarbone. For whatever reason, instead of loading me into the car, my parents called an ambulance — probably because I was screaming like a big baby and refusing to let anyone touch me. EMTs arrived. One rode in the back of the ambulance with my mom and me, and…oh my God. Blue eyes, black hair, dimple when he smiled. So stunning I can still picture him after all these years. He was also extremely patient and reassuring. Suddenly, instead of bawling my eyes out, I was tongue-tied, except to stutter, "almost eight!" when my mom told him I was seven. As if.

Thus commenced my adoration of EMTs. I am pleased to report that was my one and only ride in an ambulance. Unfortunately, it was not the last time I needed an EMT.

A few years ago I took my son to Fashion Island in Newport Beach. Why, I'm not sure, because hyperactive three-year-olds actually don't like to shop. They like to climb and jump, and they turn any available terrain into a climb and jump opportunity. He fell off a bench and hit his head. The next minutes were a nightmare. Blood everywhere, my little guy screaming and clinging to me so hard I couldn't get a look at the wound, and kind souls coming from every direction with napkins and paper towels that soaked through at a frightening rate. Finally, three men in blue uniforms ran up. They were EMTs from the Newport Beach Emergency Medical Services division. Within about five seconds they calmed my son, examined his cut, and assured me he wasn't bleeding out from his head. A few stitches and he'd be good as new. One trip to the ER and five head staples later, we were on our way. He is good as new, and my EMT crush evolved into something deeper, involving respect and admiration... and, well, still a good dose of adoration.

I hope a measure of that comes through in Beau. And I hope you enjoy him!

xoxo,
Sam

To emergency medical technicians everywhere.
Thank you for doing what you do.

Chapter One

Was it possible to be castrated by a playlist?

Beau Montgomery held his tongue while Alanis Morissette growled her way through "You Oughta Know." He basted turkey and tuned out Beyoncé's "Irreplaceable," but he refused to silently endure Gloria Gaynor's "I Will Survive." That, ladies and gentlemen, constituted disco, and he sure as hell would not survive. He was stressed enough about hosting his mom and dad for Thanksgiving dinner without the marathon set of breakup anthems coming from his neighbor's apartment.

A glance at the clock on the stove made him wince. The 'rents had left Magnolia Grove at noon. Assuming reasonable holiday traffic coming through Atlanta, they'd be on his doorstep anytime. The sexy little blonde across the hall needed to take the volume down several notches, or better yet, conclude her Men Suck Festival altogether.

Since it had been going on all day, he doubted either option would come to pass without a word from him. She probably assumed he wasn't home. He usually worked the holidays to give the other paramedics on the crew—the ones with wives and kids—a chance to spend time with their families. Even when he was home, he preferred to keep to himself. If his parents weren't part of today's equation, he'd just focus on the football games and ignore the music.

Beau cursed. Confronting her with a noise complaint on Thanksgiving felt like an asshole move, given they'd barely said hello to each other since she'd moved into the complex six months ago. She wasn't around a lot—thankfully— because when she spent time at home, she managed to disturb his peace just by existing.

She liked to sing in the shower, seemingly unconcerned if her low, Southern-bluesy voice carried, inviting him to picture her wet and naked. She liked to bake, and the hobby sent distracting scents of cinnamon and vanilla into his apartment like unwanted guests. She liked sex—thin walls held no secrets—though by his count the guy she had it with only brought her all the way home once in every three times at bat. Sheer laziness in his opinion, and why she settled for less than a grand slam every single time he really couldn't fathom. Maybe silk ties and snappy suits compensated for a lack of bedroom skills?

Or not. Today's music selections suggested she and One-for-Three had parted ways. She'd stormed into her apartment last night and proceeded to bang around as if she were rearranging furniture and digging through closets. The back-and-forth of footsteps in the hall indicated she'd made several trips to the garbage chute. He didn't need a degree in psychology to know there was a purge going on next door, both tangible and emotional.

Not that it was any of his business.

Her wild tumble of honey-blonde waves was none of his business either, but it always caught his eye, as did the playful bounce of her full, round breasts when she descended the stairs or the sway of her hips when she climbed them. Nature had stacked some truly awe-inspiring curves onto her slender five-foot-nothing frame.

Her smile usually made an appearance when they passed. She probably aimed for friendly, but something about the way those lips tilted upward in an inherently flirtatious greeting teased his cock, even on those occasions when she had One-for-Three on her arm.

Beau shook his head and went back to straightening up his kitchen. At a different point in his life, her distracting smile—or her equally distracting ass—might have tempted him to find out if she liked *his* smile, his ass, or anything in between, but that point had come and gone several years ago. He wasn't looking to get involved, no matter how strong and persistent a pull he felt toward his sexy little neighbor.

His eyes strayed to the pile of yesterday's mail he'd tossed on the counter. The mail carrier had accidentally included an item for number 202 in his box. He fanned the pile out until he spotted the embossed envelope from the Solomon Foundation for Art, which he'd never heard of. Not surprising, considering he knew fuck-all about art, but he knew a good strategy when he saw one. He'd wander over, knock on her door, and she'd have to lower the music to answer. While he delivered what probably amounted to fancy junk mail, he'd casually mention he expected his folks to arrive at any moment, and he looked forward to having a nice, *quiet* visit with them.

Satisfied with the plan, he folded the envelope, slid it into the back pocket of his jeans, and walked out his door.

The music gained volume as soon as he stepped into the hall, and he immediately understood why it seemed especially loud today. Her front door hung open, with a Post-it note on the outside reading, "Come in."

Not smart. They lived in a secure building, with nice,

normal neighbors, but still. Why court trouble?

"Hello?" He barely heard himself over the sound of Carrie Underwood and her Louisville Slugger. After pushing the door all the way open, he tried again, louder. "Hey?"

Still nothing, although judging by the scents of cooking turkey and cooling pie filling the apartment, the chef hovered nearby. Her living room and kitchen, which were mirror images of his in terms of layout, but universes apart in terms of color and texture and…stuff, were empty. Empty of people, at any rate. Her floors sported the same neutral wood laminate as his, but the rest of the room looked like a combination of Buckhead estate sale and third-world bazaar. Yet it worked. A slipcovered white sofa and a couple of matching armchairs provided a blank canvas for red throw pillows, a wrought iron coffee table straight off a French Quarter patio, and a blue-and-white ceramic garden stool stacked with old books. Atop the coffee table sat a huge glass bowl full of fist-sized marbles swirled with every hue imaginable. The arrangement made him think of exotic planets suspended in a crystalline galaxy.

An eclectic collection of art covered the walls. Large abstract oil paintings surrounded by black-and-white photographs, a few pastel watercolors, and even some framed architectural renderings.

The envelope in his back pocket started to feel less like junk mail.

The music blasted from a digital speaker dock on a long mirrored table against the wall opposite the sofa. He let that be for now and made his way down the hallway.

The bedroom door stood ajar, and he could hear her singing on the other side. He might have hesitated, but a woman with a welcome note stuck to her open front door on Thanksgiving Day clearly expected company.

"Hello…?"

He pushed the door open. It slammed into something

and swung back at him. His shoulder took the blow, and instinct had him shoving through. Whatever was on the other side gave way under the force of his momentum. He heard a scream over the last ominous lines of "Before He Cheats" and stepped into the room in time to realize he'd banged into a ladder—one on which his neighbor perched, now struggling for balance. Time slipped into a frustrating slow motion as he reached out to grab the rungs and stabilize her. Another scream assaulted his eardrums and the ladder lurched out of his reach. His neighbor fell hard on the white tarp covering the floor. She looked up at him with wide blue eyes and opened those fantasy-worthy lips to speak just as yellow droplets showered down on him.

Then the lights went out.

• • •

Maybe next time he'll think before he cheats…

The *thunk* of a nearly full can of paint meeting skull echoed in the silence between "Before He Cheats" and "Hit the Road Jack." Savannah Smith watched, stunned, as her hot neighbor's eyes glazed, and then slowly rolled up behind the descending curtains of his eyelids.

He took one swaying step backward.

Shit. She lunged forward, hands skidding through puddles of paint as she tried to catch him. One palm bounced off a hard-muscled thigh, and the other brushed the front of his jeans. No good. The man fell like an uprooted redwood.

"Oh my God!" Adrenaline helped her hurdle the capsized ladder, and she crouched beside him.

One minute she'd been painting an accent wall of her bedroom Mitchell Prescott III's least favorite color and fantasizing about slashing holes in all four tires of his pampered Audi coup. The next, she'd been strangling a scream as a looming figure swung through her door and knocked her off the ladder. An instant after she'd hurled the paint can at his head she'd recognized the intruder as her strong, silent neighbor across the hall.

Drops of yellow now spattered the planes and angles of a face she usually sneaked a second glance at when they passed. It was worth a second glance—the masculine slant of his forehead, the straight slope of his nose, and the angle of his jaw. He owned the kind of bone structure that made her wish she sculpted.

Once upon a time she might have felt a twinge of guilt at how easily his guarded eyes drew hers, or the renegade flutter the whole formidable package inspired—especially when he wore his paramedic uniform. But enjoying a harmless spark of attraction from afar ranked way down on her list of relationship transgressions. Acting on the attraction? Different story, though as she discovered last night, apparently Mitch abided by a separate set of rules.

I'm going to marry the partner's daughter. But don't worry. Nothing between us has to change.

A splattering of paint didn't camouflage number 204's good looks, or...*uh-oh*...the stream of red trickling along his temple from the gash at his hairline. Some heretofore undiscovered Florence Nightingale instinct had her pressing the hem of her black henley to the wound. Maybe she pressed too hard, because he groaned, and his hands jumped from their resting places by his hips.

"Uhhh..." His voice rumbled up from beneath her shirt, and the wash of warm breath against her torso alerted her to the fact their position gave him an under-the-tent view of her black lace bra. The bra she'd worn last night because she'd fully expected Mitch to pop the question, and she'd wanted to make the rest of the night equally memorable. Oh, he'd had a proposal for her, sure enough—one she hoped he choked on.

Another low groan pulled her attention to the present, and the man on her bedroom floor. She yanked her shirt away from her neighbor's forehead, tugged up the slipping waistband of her black thermals, and stared into platter-sized pupils floating in amber irises.

He raised his hand to wipe paint off her cheek. "You okay?"

Thanks to the volume of the music, she read his lips more than heard his voice. "I'm fine," she shouted. "Are *you* okay?"

He nodded, but she didn't like how he paled from the slight movement. Nor did she like the amount of blood flowing from the cut. "I'll be right back," she mouthed, and scooted into the attached bathroom to grab a towel.

She returned to find him shirtless, propped in a sitting position, with one hand braced behind him, and the other holding his bundled-up navy blue button-down to his forehead.

The sight left *her* a little dizzy. Even sitting on the floor he radiated strength, from his mountain range of shoulders, to his wide chest and rippling abs bracketed by a "V" cut that made her thighs clench.

Her heart might be broken, but the rest of her, including both eyes and every single one of her hormones, remained in full working order. They appreciated how his obliques sloped and narrowed, funneling her gaze down to his—

Hey, how about you ogle him later, when he's not bleeding?

"Here." She knelt beside him, tossed his shirt aside, and pressed the white towel to his cut. When he leaned into her touch, her worry doubled. During the six months she'd lived at Camden Gardens, she'd formed the impression the man rarely leaned on anyone. Not that he wasn't friendly, but "polite" defined him better. He held doors. He yielded the right-of-way on the stairs. He greeted neighbors with a brief nod.

Visitors were rare. Occasionally another paramedic came by — a gorgeous blond guy with an indecently charming grin — but no women. Based on those facts, her downstairs neighbor, Steven, insisted number 204 played for Team Rainbow. She didn't want to dash Steve's dreams, but the flash of pure male appreciation she'd noticed more than once in her reserved neighbor's broody gaze told her exactly which team he played for — or *would* play for, if he bothered playing. As far as she could tell, he'd benched himself.

All of which made his out-of-the-blue appearance in her apartment more curious, but she could wait to satisfy her curiosity until he'd stopped hemorrhaging. Something he showed no signs of doing.

Poinsettia red bloomed through the white terry cloth, and the sight sent her heart on a long, fast roller-coaster plunge into her stomach. She needed to get him off the floor, find her phone, and call 911.

Her bed stood just a few steps away. Could she drag two hundred pounds of rock-solid male a couple feet? Maybe, if the male cooperated. She wrapped her arms around him and lifted. "Come on," she groaned into his ear over the strains of "Hey Bartender." Whoa, he smelled good. Like fresh-cut juniper…she sniffed again…grown in an oak forest, and stored in freshly soaped leather. She had to resist burying her nose against his neck and inhaling deep. "Let's get you to the bed."

Lady Antebellum drowned out his reply, but he slung the towel over his shoulder and braced his hands on the paint-slicked drop cloth. Then he flexed his long legs and helped her guide him to his feet. She barely reached his chin, which made the prospect of steering him to her bed somewhat daunting, but she backed him up a step, then another, and then, with her target in sight, she got overly ambitious and took the next step too quickly. She stumbled into him and unbalanced them both. His hands came out to catch her as they fell.

The music stopped.

They landed in a tangle of limbs on her bed, her fingers hooked into the waistband of his jeans, her breast cupped in one big, wide palm, and another hand that most definitely didn't belong to her splayed across her ass.

"Hello, sweetie. We're early!" an all-too-familiar voice chirped from the hallway.

Savannah looked over to see her mother's smiling face appear at the bedroom door.

"Happy Thanks"—the smile faltered—"giving?"

"Mom!"

Savannah scrambled off her neighbor, inadvertently elbowing his unyielding abdomen in the process. Her mom inched into the room, followed by her sister, Sinclair, and her father. Three sets of eyes took in the Sun Shower wreck of her bedroom, the man sprawled across her bed, and then, strangely, the front of her shirt.

A weirdly fatalistic calm settled over her as she followed their gazes. Yep, a large, starkly yellow handprint decorated her left breast, and she had a sneaking suspicion the seat of her pants bore a similar mark. The voice of one of her more strident art school professors echoed in her head. *I don't care if you work with oils, charcoal, or garbage. Medium is irrelevant. You can create profound art with finger paint, as long as the result sends a message to the viewer.*

This certainly sent a message. Something along the lines of, "Oops. My family just interrupted my X-rated paint job." She switched her attention to the artist in question, still stretched across her mattress in bare-chested glory, propped on one elbow as if he spent all his free time languishing in her bed. Her gaze continued down his body and she swallowed a groan. Smaller but equally vivid handprints glowed against the wash-faded denim of his jeans, on the thigh, and...*oh, nice aim, Savannah*...the fly.

Her father cleared his throat—a sure sign he was preparing to speak—but she cut him off. "This isn't what it looks like."

Sinclair's midnight-blue eyes sparkled. "I don't think there's a name for what this looks like, but I take it last night's dinner went well. If you'd responded to any of the texts I sent, we would have driven slower." Her eyes slid to the bed, and she winked. "Much slower."

Crap. Sinclair assumed the half-naked man in her bed was Mitch. *That's what you get for jumping the gun yesterday afternoon and telling her you thought your six-month anniversary dinner with "M" might end with a ring.*

Old habit. Growing up, she and her sister had always been each other's closest confidants. When she'd secretly crushed on Mr. Casey, her sixth-grade art teacher. After she'd given up her V-card on a freshman year spring break trip to Fort Lauderdale. When she'd expected the ambitious-yet-romantic lawyer she'd been seeing to pop the question. Every time, she'd told Sinclair.

Her mother stepped toward the bed, her chin-length blonde curls swinging as she smiled and held out her hand.

Somebody had raised him right, because he straightened and shook her outstretched hand.

"Hello. I'm Savannah's mother, Laurel. You must be the mysterious M we've heard so much about. I'm...oh my goodness, you're bleeding."

God, he was. Still. Though not as copiously as before. He needed medical attention, not a round of introductions to her misguided family. "I told you this isn't what it looks like. I—he—"

"I surprised your daughter while she was painting." He covered the wound with the towel. "We had a minor accident."

His deep, calm voice sounded reassuringly steady, despite

the head injury, but she didn't plan on taking any chances. "Not so minor. He lost consciousness for a moment. I was about to call 911 when you arrived."

"That's not necessary," he replied.

"Absolutely not," her father seconded, his nod of agreement sending a wing of dark hair over his brow. "We'll drive you to the emergency room." He dug into the pocket of his khakis for his car keys. From the corner of her eye, Savannah caught a movement by the bedroom door, but before she could say anything, her dad added, "It's the least we can do for our future son-in-law."

"Future son-in-law?" The gasped question preceded an attractive and vaguely familiar brunette into the bedroom. She clung to the doorknob for support and blinked back tears. "Sweet baby Jesus, my secret prayers have been answered."

Chapter Two

Shit.

Beau actually felt himself turn as white as the towel he still held to his head. "Mom…Dad," he added as his father stepped into the room and wrapped an arm around his mom's shoulders. His dad looked around, gave everyone a slow smile, and said, "Howdy, strangers."

Savannah's mother squealed—there was no other word for it—and ran forward to embrace his parents. Her father followed and clapped his dad on the shoulder. "Small world."

Either he'd taken a much harder hit than he thought, or his loud, distracting, and ridiculously sexy neighbor hid a secret portal to the twilight zone in her bedroom.

"Cheryl and Trent Montgomery, is it really you?" Savannah's mother asked as she hugged his mom like a long-lost sister.

"In the flesh," his mom answered, somewhere between laughter and tears. "Laurel Smith, I'd recognize you and Bill anywhere. You two haven't aged a day."

The names rang a bell in the back of his mind. Years ago—

before he'd started first grade—they'd lived next door to a family named Smith, but when his dad had accepted a work transfer, they'd moved to California. A blurry, early memory took shape. Sneaking through adjoining backyards, leaping out at a little blonde girl and brandishing his favorite, most lifelike rubber snake in her face. He remembered a satisfyingly terrified scream followed by an interminable time-out.

He pulled his attention away from his parents and eyed the walking temptation he'd been avoiding since she moved in. Savannah Smith. Apparently they'd been neighbors before. Maybe this detail would have come to light sooner if they'd done more than nod hello to each other, but they hadn't, which made the engagement assumption their parents had leaped to downright laughable—except setting everyone straight and watching the joy and relief drain out of his parents' faces wouldn't be so funny.

"I can't believe it," Savannah's mom went on. "What brings you here?"

"We jumped on the chance to return to our roots and live closer to Beau," his father said. "We moved back to Magnolia Grove earlier this month, but between work, the move, and"— he gave his wife a squeeze—"a couple other challenges, we've been inexcusably slow about looking up old friends."

Other challenges. His father had a gift for understatement.

Savannah's mom waved a hand. "Your old friends understand completely. But what are you doing *here*, in Savannah's apartment?"

"We saw the open door and thought this was Beau's apartment," his mom explained, and then continued in a quavering voice. "When we accepted his invitation to Thanksgiving dinner, we had no clue about the surprise in store for us. Beau and Savannah...engaged." She blinked, sniffled, and lost the new battle with her tears. "I can't even tell you what this news means to us. Especially just now."

Shit. Shit… Fuck it. In the half second it took to string three curses together, he made up his mind. It might be the stupidest decision he'd ever come to, but he owed his parents a happy, worry-free Christmas—at least free of worry about him. Their families thought they were engaged, and he intended to let them keep right on thinking it until after the holidays.

Sinclair elbowed Savannah. "Now I understand why you were so freaking secretive about *M*. Well-played, you two, orchestrating a surprise reunion and an engagement announcement in one Thanksgiving dinner."

Savannah's attention swung from her sister to him, silently asking which one of them should correct the picture.

As discreetly as possible, he shook his head.

Her lips thinned. Clearly, she didn't take the hint. "We didn't plan any of this—"

Fuck discreet. He cleared his throat to drown her out and slumped against her pillow. "Sorry to interrupt the reunion, but unless everyone in this room has a twin standing next to them, I think the ER might be a good call after all."

• • •

Beau's words activated everyone. His father stepped forward to help his son to his feet. Her mother grabbed Mrs. Montgomery's hand. "I'll drive. Cheryl, you navigate. Savannah, ride in the back with Beau and keep an eye on him."

Her father took Beau's other side. "We'll follow in our car," he added as the dads walked Beau to the door.

Savannah couldn't seem to shift herself into gear, and remained parked in the middle of her bedroom. "Wait. I have dinner in the oven. Give me a second to—"

"I'll stay behind and take care of it," Sinclair said while she snagged Savannah's paint-splotched silver evening clutch and matching heels from under the bed and handed them to her. Then she whispered, "You could have told *me*. I know how to keep a secret."

Maybe, but little sis had apparently blabbed the tidbit about her expectations for last night's dinner, and now she had to manage not only her own disappointment, but that of her parents…and her neighbor's parents, which would be substantial, judging by the happy tears coursing down Mrs. Montgomery's cheeks and the ear-to-ear smile stretched across Mr. Montgomery's face. She could understand his parents' surprise, but why were they reacting like an engagement was some kind of miracle? What was wrong with this guy?

Sinclair nudged her. Right. Miracle or not, he needed a doctor. She slipped the heels on, took the clutch, and immediately flashed back to giving the shoes and purse a haphazard toss in her haste to peel herself out of her perfect "pop the question" dress last night after arriving home empty-handed, with Mitch's version of a proposal still ringing in her ears.

Up until yesterday she'd been able to tell herself life wasn't a total disaster. The big, sparkling career opportunity that had enticed her to Atlanta from Athens had flamed out—and burned her good in the process—but at least her personal life had looked promising. Looks, as it turned out, could be deceiving.

"Sinclair," Beau called over his shoulder while the dads maneuvered him out of the room. "My apartment is next door, and I've got stuff in the oven, too."

"No worries. I can handle double duty." She tugged Savannah down the hall and whispered, "Neighbors. So cute. Is that how you two met…er…reconnected?"

"Yes. I mean no." She took a breath and tried again. "I mean, yes, he's my neighbor, but I wouldn't say we reconnected."

Sinclair stopped at the front door, squeezed Savannah's

arm, and released her. "Aw. Was it like you'd known each other all along? I expect to hear every detail when you get back from the hospital."

"Savannahhhhh," her mother called from the stairwell. "It's chilly outside. Could you bring Beau a shirt?"

"Cooooming." She shook her head at Sinclair, as if one simple gesture could magically melt the snowballing assumptions coming at her from every direction, and hurried into his apartment.

She zipped through to the bedroom, barely pausing to tug a black flannel shirt off a hanger in a frighteningly organized closet before rushing to catch up with the rest of the group. Still, her artist's eye translated her surroundings into thoughts. *Sparse. Tidy. Impersonal.* This guy took minimalism to the extreme.

The ride to the hospital passed in a blur. She helped Beau into the shirt, ridiculously sad to watch his breathtaking array of muscles disappear behind a veil of flannel. Her hormones did a shameful little cheer when he abandoned his one-handed buttoning to basically drive from the backseat, relaying directions to her mom with remarkable clarity for a guy clutching a towel to his bleeding head. Then again, given his job, he could probably find the hospital blindfolded.

At least someone kept his attention on the road. Her mom's eyes continuously strayed, connecting with hers in the rearview mirror. They brimmed with questions. When she pulled into the hospital parking lot, she said, "I predicted this. Way back when Beau was barely a newborn and I found out Bill and I were having a girl, I said, 'I'll bet they end up married.'"

Mrs. Montgomery smiled back at them, still wiping tears off her cheeks.

Savannah couldn't take it anymore. *Someone* had to set everyone straight, and apparently it was going to be her. But then Beau put his hand on her knee—a warm, steady, thought-derailing hand—and said, "Mom, everything's fine. Please stop crying."

"I can't help it, honey. I'm just so happy. Not about your head, of course, but about you and Savannah."

"Mrs. Montgomery, Mom—"

"Can you let us off up here at the ER entrance?" The hand on her knee tightened as Beau spoke. Probably a reflex on his part to fight the pain, but the latent power inherent in the unconscious show of strength blindsided her with all kinds of inappropriate thoughts. That hand, tightening on her bare skin, parting her knees, and then slowly sliding up her thigh… Jeez, she'd kept this attraction corked for half a year, but half a day after things with Mitch imploded, the genie was out of the bottle. And the genie was horny as hell.

Now you know what six months of mediocre sex does to a girl.

Her mom skidded to a stop at the red curb, jostling a groan out of Beau and forcing him to move his hand from her knee to the seat back to keep from lurching forward.

He recovered fast, because he was out of the SUV before Savannah even unlatched her seat belt. She bounded out after him, wobbling a little in the high heels, and inwardly cringing at her ensemble. Paint-splotched black thermals featuring compromising handprints, and silver peekaboo stilettos. Whatever. They'd surely seen worse at the ER.

She slid under his right arm while his mom took the left. A black sedan pulled up to the curb behind the Navigator, and her dad stepped out.

"Here, let me." He switched places with Mrs. Montgomery. "Cheryl, go on ahead and get him signed in. We'll be right behind you." Tires squealed against asphalt as her mom pulled away. Savannah and her father walked Beau through the automatic doors leading to the nearly empty emergency room.

The registration clerk recognized Beau, which probably accounted for why they were whisked into an exam room immediately. A moment later her mom and Mr. Montgomery joined them, and she found herself sitting on the exam table, hip-to-hip with Beau, while questions and congratulations from both sets of parents swirled around them.

Her attention fixed on the wide, capable hand once again resting on her knee. His fingertips brushed along the waffled cotton of her leggings. Heat from the seemingly casual touch seeped through the barrier and burned her skin.

"You two win the Jack Bauer award for covert ops."

Mr. Montgomery's comment provoked laughter and some good-natured speculation from the peanut gallery. She shifted uncomfortably, and Beau's arm brushed the side of her breast. His slow inhale made her think maybe he had gotten a gander at the girls in their black lace finery while she'd used the hem of her shirt to tend to his cut. *At least somebody enjoyed the view*. Despite the cynical thought, the notion sent a wave of tingles through her—all the way from the arches of her feet to the tips of her breasts. Goose bumps rose on her forearms.

"I hope you're not planning on a long engagement."

Beau answered her mom by saying they hadn't given the matter any thought, which was true, but misleading. She raised her eyes to find his, but the yellow stamp of her handprint on the thigh of his jeans claimed her attention, and she nearly shivered at the memory of granite muscles under supple denim.

"What do you think about a spring wedding in Magnolia Grove?" his mom wanted to know.

"And the reception at the country club," her mom added. "Whitney Sloan had her reception there, remember, Bill? She had all those little paper lanterns in the trees."

Cheryl sighed. "Sounds magical…"

Without permission, Savannah's eyes searched out the other handprint, and widened at the impressive ridge forming behind the comparatively dainty impression. Her throat went dry, and her palm suddenly itched.

Beau's soft groan barely reached her ears. He casually widened his legs until the tail of his shirt slipped down to cover his fly.

"How soon will I get a grandbaby?"

The last question startled her out of her stupor. "Mom!"

He squeezed her knee again. She looked up at him in time to see a muscle tick in his jaw, and then a new voice broke into the chaos.

"Folks, I'm Dr. West, and I hate to break up the party, but I need two-thirds of the population of this room to relocate to the waiting area."

Savannah swiveled her head to find a middle-aged African-American woman in dark blue scrubs framed by the doorway. She started to jump down from the table, but the hand on her knee held her in place. Their parents moved to the door instead, and funneled out under the doctor's watchful eye, still immersed in talk of weddings and grandchildren.

"Montgomery, you are the last ugly white boy I expected to see in my ER today."

He found a smile for her. "Delilah, you know I can't stay away from you."

"Hmm. Don't be sweet-talking me when you've got a pretty young thing sitting beside you." She rolled her eyes and grinned at Savannah. "Some men have absolutely no game. Honey"—she approached, wrapped a paper bracelet around Beau's wrist, and motioned for him to move the towel—"what craziness did this fool resort to just to get your attention?"

"It's my fault," Savannah answered, her guilt mounting as the doctor frowned at the gash. "He surprised me and I accidentally knocked him in the head with a paint can. He lost consciousness."

"I was stunned for a second."

"You lost consciousness. He could have a concussion or...I don't know...brain damage." Otherwise, he'd have already put the kibosh on the ridiculous engagement misunderstanding.

Light brown eyes narrowed and cut to her. "I don't have brain damage."

Dr. West clicked her tongue and gingerly tipped his head down to more closely examine the wound. "Heck no, sugar. You'd have to have a brain first, which you clearly do not, seeing as how you don't know better than to sneak up on a person." She patted his shoulder. "You're going to need stitches for sure, but I want to get a CT before we close you up." She made her way to the door. "Sit tight. Someone will be in to take you down to radiology soon."

And then they were alone, for what felt like the first time. Her and this near-stranger—a man both sets of parents believed to be the love of her life, her husband-to-be, not to mention the father of her unborn children. How had things spiraled out of control so quickly?

She looked down. The yellow handprint on the front of her shirt filled her vision. Oh, yeah. There was that. She slid off the table and tried adjusting the henley, but no matter how she arranged the fabric, the stamp of his large hand found its way back to her breast. Resigned, she turned to face him. "I'll go set them straight."

He raised his head. His gaze landed on the imprint of his palm on her shirt and turned hot. Her chest tightened. The heated inspection continued up her throat, and stalled again at her mouth. She couldn't keep from licking her lips. Slowly, inevitably, those amber eyes found hers—like double shots of Johnnie Walker Gold, and twice as potent.

"Don't."

Chapter Three

"Don't what?"

If his neighbor suspected he had brain damage before, she looked damn near certain of it now. He needed to talk fast or she'd be in the lobby letting the cat out of the bag before he made it back from getting his head examined.

"Don't set them straight."

Her eyes widened, and her mouth dropped open. Her expression suggested she'd revised his status from brain damaged to insane. And maybe he was out of his mind at the moment, but the sight of one's mother dissolving into grateful tears and praising Jesus impacted a guy. It also offered up a painful reminder that he wasn't the only one who'd suffered over the last three years. His parents had, too, and along with the reminder came a shameful realization—he'd withdrawn so far into his own self-protective cave he'd inadvertently added to their pain, and heaped on an unhealthy dose of plain old worry. About him. Had the stress contributed to his mom's recent cancer diagnosis? Guilt gnawed at his gut. It certainly hadn't done her any favors. He'd been given an opportunity to alleviate that worry so his parents could shift their energy and focus to his mom's well-being. No, it wasn't honest, or strictly ethical, but it felt right.

"I know I sound crazy, but I promise I'm not. Just hear me out."

She crossed her arms, chewed her lower lip, and shot a glance at the door. He estimated he had about two seconds before she bolted. Usually he went to great lengths to avoid talking about the past. The conversation left him raw all over again, but right now showing his ugliest scars served a purpose.

"Three years ago, almost to the day, I lost my wife and baby daughter in a car accident."

That snapped her attention back to him. "Oh my God. I'm so sorry."

And she was. He could see the emotion swimming in her eyes, feel it in the light touch of her hand on his.

An awkward silence stretched. Three years and he still didn't know what to do with people's sympathy. "Thanks," he finally managed. "The months following the accident were"—he grappled for a word to describe the hopelessness, the rage, and the unbearable pain of loss—"hell. For all of us."

"Of course they were." Her soft voice barely exceeded a whisper. No platitudes, no advice, just acceptance of the truth of the statement. She squeezed his hand as she said the words, and he fought the strangest urge to wrap his arms around her and hold on.

"Things leveled out after a while. I adjusted to my new reality." He forced a smile to soften the bitterness in his voice. "A little more time passed and my parents—particularly my mom—started dropping little hints whenever we'd talk. Hints like the Hamiltons' nice, single niece recently moved to Atlanta and could probably use a tour guide, or the McKays' middle daughter finally divorced her no-good husband and accepted a teaching job at Emory, and that's not so far from you, is it?"

Her lips twisted into the off-center smile that always captivated his cock.

"Sounds familiar?"

She nodded. "Vaguely." Her grimace almost made him laugh. "They want us to be happy, but in your case, the natural instinct to meddle is compounded because—"

"Because they want to know I'm okay. Yeah, I get that now. They need assurances I'm not so trapped in the pain of the past that I'm closed off to the future. Their compulsion to be certain I'm squared away might have reached a new urgency because my mom was recently diagnosed with breast cancer."

"Jesus, Beau. Is it serious? I mean, of course it's serious, but—"

"We're hoping for the best. She caught the lump early and it's stage one, so…" Nothing more to say there until they knew more. "They don't need to waste their energy worrying about me, and I didn't understand how worried they were until this afternoon. When your father referred to me as his future son-in-law, my mother cried tears of happiness, and an invisible weight rolled off my dad. I don't want to take that away from them."

"That's very sweet and noble of you, but we can't lie to ease their minds."

"Sure we can."

She opened her mouth to rebut, but he forged ahead. "Not forever, just a few weeks. The holidays are a difficult time for us. I assumed they always would be, but now I— *we*—have a chance to restore some hope and joy to the season for my parents." Unfair of him to emphasize how his parents' happiness now rested on her narrow shoulders, but circumstances had manipulated them into this position, and not even the annoying needles of guilt over his tactics changed his mind.

She bit her lip again. He waited.

"You're only delaying their inevitable disappointment and making it more acute. Don't you think they'll take the news much harder if they spend the next month emotionally invested in our happily ever after? Plus, I don't know about your parents, but mine will be beyond pissed when they learn we lied to them."

"They'll never know about the lie. They live two hundred miles away. They only know what we tell them. Shortly after the New Year we'll reach the conclusion we make better friends than soul mates and call off the engagement. Simple and civilized."

"And then your parents will go back to worrying about you."

"No. They'll realize I'm okay, I just mistook rekindled childhood affection and"—no point pretending it wasn't there—"grown-up lust for more."

Dark blonde eyebrows arched. "Lust?"

"I got smacked in the head, Savannah, but I'm a long way from dead, which is what a man would have to be not to lust after you." As compliments went, it lacked poetry and subtlety, but her cheeks turned a lust-inspiring shade of pink anyway, and he imagined them turning the same color while her lips formed his name and her body trembled against his.

Careful, Montgomery. Acknowledging the lust was arguably strategic. Acting on it? Not. Time to sell her on this from another angle. "Look, I don't know the details of your situation, but I get the impression your family developed some expectations about your personal life, and having a fiancé for the next little while might save you some grief. Wouldn't you like to get through the holidays without awkward explanations? Especially the kind guaranteed to trigger the parental meddling instincts?"

She scrubbed the heels of her hands over her eyes, which reminded him of the trips she'd made down the hall to the garbage chute last night. She hadn't gotten much sleep.

"Yes, the notion holds some appeal, but"—she blinked and focused on him again—"it's dishonest."

"A victimless lie to serve a higher good. Everyone deserves a happy holiday. If we do this, we all win. You avoid a bunch of unwanted matchmaking efforts. I avoid the same. Your parents get to fixate on Sinclair's love life instead of yours, and my parents get some long-overdue peace of mind."

"One question."

He fought back a grin of triumph. The question was a formality. He had her. "Shoot."

"*Should* they be worried you're so trapped in the pain of the past, you're closed off to the future?"

A knee-jerk denial leaped to his lips, but her unwavering, don't-bullshit-me stare had him biting it back. He'd celebrated victory too soon. Knowing this, he answered carefully. "I've come to terms with the past. Maybe not willingly, or gracefully, but ultimately I didn't have much choice. As for the future, I take it as it comes, because, again, I don't have much choice. I prefer to concentrate on the present."

Those blue eyes softened with sympathy, but her mouth turned down in a slight frown. "That doesn't really answer my question."

Did she expect him to say he had the capacity to put his heart and soul on the line again, risk standing by helplessly while whatever power controlled such things ripped everything he loved away from him? He did not. He'd lived through it once, and just in case time tried to heal the wound, his job presented him with regular reminders of how fragile all those hopes and dreams were when pitted against the whims of fate. Did that qualify him as closed off, or sane? Probably both. Either way, he knew his limits.

"I'm fine. Nobody needs to worry about me."

She continued to nibble her lower lip as she considered him, and he momentarily lost himself in a fantasy of sinking his teeth into the soft swell.

"Hey, Montgomery. West told me you decided to spend Thanksgiving with me."

He looked over to see a young, spike-haired orderly at the door with a wheelchair.

"Don't flatter yourself, Isaiah. My plans didn't include you."

The kid grinned, showing off a gold-crowned front tooth, and pushed the chair into the room. "Planned or not, I'm here to wheel your sorry ass to radiology."

Savannah took a couple steps toward the door. "I'll just… ah…go out to the waiting room."

Shit. Would she tell their families the truth? He tried to read her intentions as Isaiah cornered him with the chair, but he didn't know her well enough to guess what the little crinkle between her eyebrows meant. Assuming he enjoyed any advantage whatsoever, now seemed like the time to press it.

"Don't leave me at this guy's mercy." He took a seat in the wheelchair and hit her with the best pleading look he could manage. "He's lost more patients in these hallways than I can count."

Isaiah rolled his eyes. "Two lousy patients in four years, and they were both deliberate runners. Neither was my fault."

"One ended up in the morgue."

"Don't make it sound like that. Dude got lost, not dead—"

"God knows where I'll end up." Beau angled his chin down and looked up at her from under his eyelashes. "Chaperone me. There's a waiting area in radiology."

"I don't want to break any rules…" Her uncertain gaze shifted to Isaiah.

The orderly shrugged. "No rule against accompanying this wussy-assed whiner to X-ray. Personally, I think this has nothing to do with me, or my supposedly *lost* patients. More like big bad Beau Montgomery freaks out at the thought of sticking his noggin in a tube. But if it calms his nerves to have a pretty lady holding his sweaty hand while he waits, that's okay with me."

Beau bit his tongue. He had no qualms about the CT, but if compassion kept her at his side, he'd play along. "I'd appreciate the company, if you don't mind."

Her off-center smile tugged on his balls. "Of course I don't mind." To Isaiah, she added, "Lead the way."

The heels of her silver…stilettos? pumps?—he didn't know what to call them—tapped along the marbleized linoleum as she walked beside him. Her fuck-me shoes from her date last night, he decided, and experienced a strange surge of satisfaction knowing One-for-Three had fucked nothing but himself.

They turned right at an intersection of corridors, and followed the signs to the radiology department. Isaiah wheeled him into the waiting area, paused at the reception desk to drop his version of a charming smile on the admin minding the desk, and then sent him a salute along with a pithy, "So long, sucka," on his way out.

Savannah took an empty seat beside his chair. "I'm sorry I conked you in the head."

He waved off the apology. "It's not like you saw me coming and took aim. I frightened you. You obeyed a standard reflex to defend yourself."

The crinkle reappeared between her eyes. "You know, I still have no idea what brought you to my apartment in the first place."

Admitting he'd come over with a noise complaint seemed counterproductive. "Maybe I wanted to borrow a cup of sugar?"

"Ha. You're not exactly the borrow-a-cup-of-sugar kind of neighbor. The entire time I've lived next door we've exchanged less than three words. I never dreamed you were the same lady-killer who tried to impress me when I was five by riding his bike no-handed and ended up crashing into the garage door."

Oh, yeah, he'd done that, hadn't he? Her little laugh fluttered the fine hairs on his arm. He imagined her breath ruffling other sensitive zones, and shifted in the chair as his jeans turned into a self-inflicted bondage game. "Did it work?"

"I might have had a weakness for risk-takers back then, but I know better now. We've both changed a lot since those days." Her eyes drifted down his body, provoking an instant response from a part of him still eager to impress her, and then snapped up to meet his. "A *lot*. We definitely don't know each other well enough to convince our families we're engaged."

His hard-on backed off. Mentioning the lie he hoped to perpetrate on their families had that effect on him. The good news? She was still considering the deception. The bad news? She had a point. But not an insurmountable one. "You're Savannah Smith: snake hater, lover of yellow walls and black lace."

She laughed. "Well, okay, I stand corrected. You got me in a nutshell. But for the record, I haven't forgotten about you chasing me around our backyards, terrorizing me with that creepy rubber snake. I'm afraid we have irreconcilable differences."

His lips threatened to stretch into a smile. "How can you say that to the man who gave you your first flowers?" He remembered picking daisies with her in the backyard.

"Those were your mom's flowers, and they don't make up for the snake."

"Not so fast, Smith. I outgrew the snakes some time ago."

"'Round about the time you developed an appreciation for black lace?"

"A man's interests evolve. I can go either way on yellow

walls, if that helps."

"Very accommodating of you." Her smile lingered, though he still saw plenty of reservations lurking in those clear blue eyes. "You really think you know me well enough to pull this off?"

"We just have to make it through this afternoon. After that, like I said, our parents live a safe distance away so it's not like we have to keep this up on a day-in-day-out basis until January. As far as today goes, I think you're underestimating my powers of observation."

"Okay, Sherlock, tell me something about me."

He racked his brain for details. The piece of mail tucked in his back pocket sprang to mind. He retrieved the embossed envelope from the Solomon Foundation for Art, and held it out to S.E. Smith in apartment number 202. "You're into art."

"Yes. What's this?"

"The mail carrier put it in my box yesterday by mistake."

She took the envelope and slipped it into her purse. "Misdirected mail brought you to my apartment this afternoon? You could have slipped it in my box."

"Mail delivery was my cover, to further my real goal of getting you to lower your music."

"Oh." Her cheeks colored a bit. "Sorry. I didn't realize I was disturbing you. I guess I got caught up in my redecorating."

"I figured something along those lines. I heard you moving stuff around last night, too."

"Crap, I'm really sorry. I don't mean to win the most annoying neighbor award. I'm usually not so loud. Especially at night."

Not purposely, no, but the echo of her voice through the wall replayed in his mind. Breathless snippets of, *That's good. A little more. Almost...almost...oh, no, not yet...*

"You'd be surprised how well sound travels. Especially at night."

Chapter Four

Exactly *what* sounds traveled surprisingly well at night? The slightest lift of a dark brow answered her unvoiced question. Savannah smacked her palm to her overheating face and nearly groaned out loud. Dammit, wouldn't a decent neighbor give a girl a heads-up when that sort of disturbance first became apparent?

Then again, what would one say? *Hi. We haven't met, but I feel like I know you. I definitely know when you and your boyfriend have sex.*

Hiding behind both hands now, she asked, "Is it just you, or have I provided the entire complex with a cheap thrill?"

"Just me. I'm the only one with a bed flush against the magic wall, and apart from when I'm lying there with no TV or music going, I don't hear much."

Thank God for small favors, but it seemed like a very small favor in the grand scheme of things. Yesterday at this time she'd been anticipating a proposal from Mitch, and a celebration of the big news over Thanksgiving dinner with her family. Today she had a trampled heart and two sets of parents ecstatic about her nonexistent engagement to a man who knew her best as the noisy sex lady next door.

She lowered her hands to her lap and offered him an apologetic smile. "If it's any interest to you, my side of the wall will be much quieter from here on out."

"I got the feeling based on today's music choices. You and One-for-Three call it quits?"

"One-for-Three?"

He shrugged. "By my count. Like I said, sound travels."

"Oh my God. You heard how often I—"

"I mostly heard how often you didn't." Something in his tone suggested he could do better. Much better.

She ought to have been mortified, but the statement, combined with his matter-of-fact expression, coaxed a laugh out of her. She reached out and patted his cheek. "Maybe I'm just a quiet storm kind of girl?"

He crossed his arms and stretched his legs so they extended beyond the footrests of the wheelchair. His dark brow lifted again. "You sing in the shower. You crank your music to eleven." Slowly, purposefully, he traced the yellow handprint stamped across the thigh of his jeans. "You even like your walls loud. You're *not* the quiet storm type."

Since when was she so easy to peg? Following some defensive instinct to throw him off balance, she lined her hand up with the imprint on his thigh. "You don't like loud?" Backfire. Of their own accord, her fingers sank into the taut muscles beneath the soft denim.

His eyes darkened, and almost reluctantly, he moved the pad of his thumb along the peaks and valleys of her knuckles, his slow, circling touch light but thorough. Mesmerizingly thorough. She imagined the same gentle massage along other, more personal peaks and valleys. The muscles in her legs dissolved, and she tightened her grip on his thigh in a useless attempt to anchor herself against a sudden wave of longing.

His touch traveled to the crevices between her splayed fingers. "I didn't say that." He slipped his thumb between her fingers and raked the edge of his nail lightly across the center of her palm. The faint scrape woke nerve endings there, and in every other area of her body where nerve cells concentrated—her scalp, the soles of her feet, and some frustratingly neglected territory south of her belly button. When his nail grazed her palm again, the tingling between her legs intensified, turning into something sharp and demanding. If her erogenous zones could speak, they'd be saying…

"Mr. Montgomery, we're ready for you."

A nurse stood at the door between the waiting area and the imaging suites.

Beau jerked his head around, and then practically sprang to his feet.

She leaped up as well and went after the chair. "Hey. Hold on. They put you in this for a reason."

He simply kept walking. The nurse stepped forward and waved Savannah back to her seat. "The ones who should know better are always the most stubborn."

"Says Miss Lettie, the queen of stubborn," he shot back, but allowed the heavyset woman to take his arm. To Savannah, he said, "Don't go anywhere," and disappeared through the door.

Go anywhere? As if her limbs would support her. She dropped back into her chair, crossed her right knee over her left, and rubbed her overstimulated palm along her leg. *Note to self. Do not pet the paramedic.*

What she needed right now was a distraction, so she opened her clutch and pulled out the letter. Her heart quickened as she spied "The Solomon Foundation for Art" in gold calligraphy in the upper left corner.

Holy shit. Was she about to catch an actual break? She tore open the envelope and unfolded the sheet of crisp ivory stationery.

Dear Ms. Smith,

Thank you for your interest in The Solomon Foundation's patronage program. After a careful review of your application, your body of work, and your project proposal, we are pleased to offer you a nine-month fellowship at our facility in Venice, Italy, commencing this January.

Her hands shook, making it hard to read the rest of the page. Compensation—yes, they'd pay her to create her most ambitious pieces to date. An apartment in the historic Solomon Palazzo adjacent to their state-of-the-art glassblowing studio. A collective of skilled hands to assist her. In short, the opportunity of a lifetime, and she could desperately use one at the moment.

She refolded the letter and returned it to her purse for safekeeping. As she did, her phone vibrated. A text from Sinclair lit the screen.

How's Beau? Everything's under control here. I cleaned up your room best I could in between basting two turkeys. How much bird do you think we eat?! Also put champagne in the fridge, because I know Mom & Dad will want to celebrate. Any ETA on when we get this party started?

Was her little sister psychic? How in God's name did she already know about the fellowship? Wait. Realization sank in as she reread the text. The celebration Sinclair referred to was for her "engagement" to Beau. She texted a thanks and told Sinclair to sit tight.

Her sister was right. Their parents did want to celebrate. A ruthlessly honest voice in her head admitted that an engagement to Mitchell Prescott III, Esq., wouldn't have generated the same unbridled enthusiasm. Magnolia Grove wasn't Mayberry, and she didn't hail from a family of bumpkins, but something about him had always struck her as a little overly ambitious for their tastes.

For hers, too, as it turned out. She'd honestly had no clue he'd been dating anyone on the side. Apparently marrying into the firm offered more upside potential than marrying a glass artist grappling with a serious career downturn.

He loved her work. That much she believed. They'd met the evening of her very first Atlanta showing when he'd purchased one of her pieces.

She'd loved him for loving it. How could she not? She literally breathed her life into her creations. They represented her in an intimate, elemental way. His respect for her artistic process, and his genuine appreciation for the result, had captured her heart. Even after her career went off the rails, his steadfast belief she'd be selected for the fellowship had bolstered her sagging confidence and made her think they understood each other on a fundamental level.

A mistake, obviously, and as a result, she'd projected other admirable qualities where none actually existed. Important qualities like integrity and fidelity.

Last night proved he possessed neither. Those deficits would have come to light eventually, but the twenty-twenty hindsight did little to ease the sting of unwittingly wasting half a year auditioning for the role of "other woman." Her blood still boiled, thinking of him sitting across the table from her in the fancy French restaurant with a smug smile on his face while calmly explaining how an attorney on the fast track to partner needed the kind of spouse who stuck close and projected the firm's proper, conservative image. Not an "unconventional artist, living in a commune in Europe."

In this case "unconventional" really meant "unsuccessful." A humbling realization for a girl who hit town wearing the crown and sash of the next big thing in the Atlanta art world, and quickly fell from grace due to circumstances beyond her control. Stupid her, thinking the potential of her receiving a fellowship half a world away had inspired him to propose, so they could spend the time apart with the security of a strong commitment in place. Instead, the manipulative weasel had twisted things around, implying that her unfortunate choice in gallery representation made it untenable for them to be together. As if her career setback sabotaged their relationship by reflecting badly on him. The man had no heart. No soul. No balls.

The mediocre sex should have told you something.

True. But she'd put his less-than-impressive…ahem… follow-through down to a teensy lack of imagination in the bedroom, and instead let his endless supply of romantic gestures dazzle her.

She'd mistaken the late candlelight dinners, flowers for no reason, and surprise getaways as indicators of his passion for her, and ignored how the sex itself had fallen short of passionate. One-for-Three — Beau's nickname for Mitch pretty much nailed it. He tended to come first, come fast, and fall asleep as soon as the deed was done. Where the hell was the passion in that?

A practical part of her had assumed they'd reached the comfortable phase of their relationship, when in fact they'd reached the nonexclusive phase. What a prick.

So be it. She shook her hair out of her face and straightened her spine, while one of her mom's favorite sayings rang in her ears. *No point crying with open eyes.* Her eyes were now wide open when it came to Mitch, and she wouldn't waste her tears on him, but she didn't look forward to disclosing the whole pathetic mess to her family.

They'd sympathize. They'd console. They'd tell her she deserved better. Then her mother would take it upon herself to find better, and dedicate the holidays to setting Savannah up with every unattached man Mom and the other Daughters of Magnolia Grove could shame into dating her.

Unless she thought you were already engaged…which she does.

Would it be so wrong to let the mistake ride until after the New Year? Her parents had raised her to tell the truth, except where doing so would needlessly injure someone's feelings. Horizontal stripes never made a friend look fat, a baked-from-scratch dinner always tasted wonderful, and no matter who soloed at Sunday service, the performance always sounded heavenly. Pretending to be engaged to Beau Montgomery for a few short weeks amounted to the same kind of little white lie, didn't it? A harmless deception. Possibly even a helpful one if it eased his parents' minds?

You're considering lying to your family, but at least stay honest with yourself. She wasn't blind or stupid. She knew hard-core lust when she felt it. Her battered ego basked in the heat of Beau's stare, and the rest of her wasn't immune, either. The simple sweep of his thumb over her palm shot her straight into a pre-orgasmic danger zone. Her pent-up body craved more than mere release. It craved complete and total salvation from the lackluster routine of the last several months. But acting on the attraction amounted to skipping through a minefield. Drunk. At midnight.

He lived next door. Their parents called the same town home. They were already waist-deep in a scheme that required they remain on friendly terms for the rest of the year, if not the rest of their lives. Then again, come January she'd board a plane to Italy, which offered a pretty decent eject button.

The door to the waiting area closed with a soft *thud*. She looked up to find Beau standing before her, his expression unreadable.

"Ready?"

The single word provoked a far-from-harmless flutter in her belly. Was she ready to leave radiology? Sure. Ready to skip through a minefield, drunk, at midnight? She didn't know.

· · ·

He stayed silent while an orderly wheeled him back to the ER. The wheelchair irked, but Beau understood hospital policy, and frankly, he figured it advanced his cause to look as harmless as possible. Especially after a simple touch in the radiology waiting room had charged the air around them with unstable chemistry.

He needed to review that whole conversation he'd had with himself about acknowledging lust versus acting on it. Acknowledging said, "It's there. I see it," much like a driver acknowledging a hazard in the road ahead. Acting on it amounted to steering straight for the hazard. Unfortunately, without meaning to, that's exactly what he'd done. Touching her had definitely been a mistake. A potentially fatal one, now that she'd had a few minutes to think about the dangers. He hoped not, but the moment called for patience, not pressure.

His patience paid off. As soon as the exam room door whooshed closed behind the departing orderly, she propped herself against the table and stared down at him. "Okay, Montgomery, exactly how do you envision us executing this brilliant scheme of yours?"

"We keep things simple. Stick to the truth as much as possible."

"With the notable exception of the whole 'we're in love and getting married' bit."

He dipped his head in concession. "Except for that."

She folded her arms and gripped her elbows as if holding herself together. "How'd we meet?"

He stood and approached her, slow and casual to counterbalance the tension coming off her. "You moved in next door." He braced a hand on the table by her hip. "And immediately caught my eye."

"Did I?" She scanned his face, and he noticed the thin black striations in her horizon-blue irises.

"Hell, yes. We got to talking, and quickly realized we knew each other from back in the day." He leaned in a little closer, drawn to the faint freckles on the bridge of her nose. He remembered those freckles. "Maybe that explains why we felt such an instant — "

"Connection?" The tip of her tongue swept over the small vee notched into the center of her upper lip.

"Attraction."

The tongue detoured to her plush lower lip, and then retreated. "Attraction's easy. Happens all the time. How did we get from attraction to love?"

"For me, it was the little things. The way you sing in the shower. The way you bite your lip when you're trying to make an important decision. The home-baked apple pie might have been a factor."

Those naked lips quirked into her tilted smile, and he silently added that to his list.

"You're good at this. But you should fall in love with my talent, too. I'm an artist. My professional name is S.E. Smith, and without her in the mix, I'm just another pretty face."

Untrue, but now wasn't a wise moment to point out all the other talents he'd noticed every time she'd gone up or down the stairs at Camden Gardens. Never would be the better time for that conversation. He straightened. "I have to confess I don't know shit about art. Give me a couple catchphrases so I don't sound like an asshat talking about how your work captures the complex, shifting essence of what it means to be human."

Her laugh eased some of the tension in the room. "Lucky for you, I went through my 'complex, shifting essence' phase years ago. I'm a glass artist."

"Right. Glass artist. I'm not sure what that means."

"I blow glass. You should come down to Glassworks Studios—that's where I rent furnace time—and see for yourself. But in the meantime, just use words like 'colorful,' 'vibrant,' and 'extremely breakable.' If you really want to impress my family, you can say my work looks like Dale Chihuly had a tempestuous affair with Queen Elsa from *Frozen*."

"You're way better than Dale Chihuahua."

His ignorance earned him another throaty laugh. "And that's why I fell for you."

"Because of my art appreciation?"

"Because you make me laugh." She fiddled with the collar of his shirt, and her smile turned sly. "Plus I like how you fill out your paramedic's uniform."

The comment surprised him. Not the flirtatiousness—he'd never mistaken her for shy—but based on her boyfriend choice, he'd pegged her for the suit-and-tie type. "I didn't realize you'd noticed."

"Are you kidding? We all noticed."

"We all?"

"Mrs. Washington in one-twenty-two—"

"Shut up. She's ninety years old."

"Nothing wrong with her eyesight. She fans her face and says, 'Oooh mercy, dat ass,' every time you walk by. And Steven in one-oh-two says next time the temperature hits triple digits, he's going to fake a swoon and hope for mouth-to-mouth." She lowered her voice to a whisper and added, "Don't tell him I divulged his plan."

As a rule, people in medical professions didn't embarrass easily, but the thought of his neighbors discussing his... assets...did the trick. "His plan contains a fundamental flaw. He has to do more than pass out to get the kiss of life."

The corners of her mouth tightened, pushing her lips into

a sexy little pout, and his lip-biting fantasy returned in full force.

"I had no idea paramedics were so stingy with the mouth-to-mouth."

"We like to play hard-to-get."

Amusement danced in her eyes. "In that case, I guess I should be flattered by your offer." She smoothed her fingers over his shoulder and down the front of his shirt, frowning slightly as her hand came to rest in the center of his chest. "There's a lot of chemistry here, but for both our sakes, we probably shouldn't act on it."

She'd read his mind. Why the relief her words should have brought felt more like irritation, he couldn't say. She'd just come out of a relationship, and if he interpreted the theme of this morning's music medley correctly, she wasn't looking to get involved again soon. His default setting was "not looking to get involved." Even if they were looking, getting involved with each other put a lot at risk. "We're on the same page," he said, and told the renegade in his jeans to calm down. "No complications."

She nodded. "Agreed. No complications." But her frown deepened. "Our families might expect an occasional display of affection."

His right palm tingled with the phantom weight of her breast, and his left hand twitched at the memory of cupping her tight, round ass. "I'm sure we can muster up something convincing."

"I don't know. You're blushing pretty hard right now just thinking about it."

"I'm blushing thinking about my pervy neighbors speculating on my mouth-to-mouth skills."

"If you say so."

The allegedly logical part of his mind insisted she had a point. "You want a demonstration?"

She tipped her face up, shook her hair back, and he caught a flowery hint of shampoo or perfume, or maybe just *her* drifting under the antiseptic hospital smell.

"A dress rehearsal might be in order. I don't mean to criticize, but the last time you kissed me, your technique needed work."

He had no idea what she was talking about, but he had a strong and unwise desire to trace every curve of her teasing grin with his tongue. See if she tasted as sweet as she smelled. "I think you're confusing me with someone else, Smith. We've never kissed before."

"My mom's got a photo that tells a different story."

Another small step on her part brought her body flush against his. The move produced a swift inhale from her, and then her eyes rounded at the evidence of what he'd *mustered* up pressing against her stomach. He found both reactions extraordinarily gratifying. She rested her palms on his chest. Having her hands on him also didn't suck. "Exactly how old was I in this alleged kissing photo?"

Her gaze traveled over his face and came to rest at his mouth. "Fairly young…and fairly naked. We both were. To be honest, if not for the nudity, I'd have a hard time telling us apart." She licked her lips.

"Well, brace yourself, Savannah. I'm all grown up, and you'll know which one is me, even with our clothes on."

Eyes locked on hers, he lowered his head. Her eyelids drifted down, her body melted into his…

"Hold up there, Romeo. This here's an ER, not a kissing booth."

Chapter Five

Dammit. His better judgment needed to get a leash on his libido, or these next few weeks would be torture. Beau reluctantly dropped his arm from Savannah's waist and stepped away as Delilah West walked into the exam room.

"That's right. Back away from the blonde. You keep your lips to yourself for the next little while and let your brain have the oxygen."

That drew his attention away from the mouth he'd been a hairbreadth from sharing oxygen with. He turned to the doc. "Seriously?"

She nodded. "'Fraid so. CT shows a little swelling. Are you scheduled to work tomorrow?"

"Yes."

"Congratulations, you've got the day off, or go in and do administrative stuff if you're like me and always have a stack of paperwork on your desk. After tomorrow, if you feel fine, you can go back in the bus."

"Shit." So much for downplaying the incident with the rest of the crew. By this time tomorrow everyone he worked with would know he'd gotten a concussion and a headful of stitches for Thanksgiving. He could already hear them talking trash and calling him Frankenstein. Heartless motherfuckers. All of them. He might as well save himself some trouble and get a middle finger tattooed on his forehead.

Delilah motioned him to the exam table and began assembling a tray of supplies to stitch up his cut. "Can someone check on you tonight? Wake you up a couple of times and make sure you know your name, date of birth, and how many fingers they're holding up?"

His parents would stay if he asked them, but his one-bedroom apartment offered no comfortable space for guests. His partner, Hunter, could crash on his couch. He'd bitch like the princess with the pea about spending a night on the sofa, but he'd do it. "Yeah, I'll get—"

"I can," Savannah said.

He glanced over at her. She wore a guilty I-gave-him-brain-damage look.

"Perfect." Delilah ran down the symptom list with Savannah while she prepped him for stiches, concluding with, "Do you want to stay while I close this up, or would you like to step out to the waiting area?"

"She'll stay." High-handed of him, yes, but he wanted to present a united front to their parents. They didn't have their story tight, and if they got out of sync, the charade would be over before they made it out of the ER.

• • •

Watching Dr. West suture a neat line of stitches along the top of Beau's forehead didn't tie a knot in Savannah's stomach. The older woman worked with the speed and efficiency of someone who knew what she was doing. Receiving the list of instructions and symptoms to keep an eye out for didn't raise her stress level much. But tendrils of tension unfurled in her stomach when Beau linked his fingers through hers and led them to the waiting room—and their parents—all of whom stood as they approached.

The moms clucked over the bandage on his forehead and the stitch count. Seven. Beau downplayed the concussion to a lingering headache, and gave her hand a thankful squeeze when she refrained from blurting out the actual diagnosis, which probably made her the world's best fake fiancée.

And a crappy fake daughter-in-law, a little voice in her head tacked on as they made their way out to the cars. Whatever. None of this was likely to earn her any honesty points, but going along with the omission seemed like the kind of thing a real fiancée might do to spare her future in-laws a sleepless night.

They re-formed their rush-to-the-hospital groups for the trip home, and Savannah spent the ride in the back of the Navigator again, buckled next to Beau. This time the moms didn't have a medical emergency to distract them, and they jumped right into information-gathering mode.

"So," Beau's mom prompted, "tell us how he popped the question."

Following his advice to stick to the truth, she responded, "Um. Very unexpectedly," and glanced sideways at him.

"Really?" Her mom's eyebrows lifted. "No need to play coy, Savannah. Sinclair told us you suspected last night's dinner would include a proposal."

Shoot. She straight up sucked at this. Less than a minute into the official spinning of the web of lies and already caught in an inconsistency of her own making.

Beau laughed and brushed her hair behind her shoulder, as if he'd performed the small, intimate gesture a thousand times before. She shivered as his fingertips lingered on the curve of her ear. "Guess I tipped my hand when I told you to wear something pretty?"

She turned to him, grateful for the rescue line. "I hoped you'd ask. I had a feeling, but I didn't take it as a foregone conclusion."

A teasing smile didn't quite overshadow the sympathy lurking in his eyes. Yes, they'd touched on her situation before, but now she was one of two people sitting in the car who realized she'd gone to dinner last night expecting to become someone's one and only, and instead came home alone. She looked away and blinked rapidly. A lump formed in her throat.

"What did you wear, honey?" her mom asked.

Beau beat her to the response while she battled the lump.

"She wore a purple dress that turned her eyes violet and turned me into the most envied man in the restaurant."

Okay, two things just became immediately apparent. He really did have amazing powers of observation, and she should let him do most of the talking, since he could come up with a line like that from a two-second glimpse of her yesterday evening when she'd passed him in the hall on her way to meet Mitch.

"Which restaurant?" This time Beau's mom posed the question.

Savannah held her tongue, waiting for him to respond, but he didn't automatically toss out a place. Maybe he wanted her to go ahead and name the actual restaurant? The silence stretched.

"Le Bistro," she blurted, at the same time Beau said, "Barcelona."

"Le Bistro Barcelona," she stammered. "It's new... French-Spanish fusion."

Beau's mother laughed and turned in her seat to beam at them. "Olé and ooh la la! Sounds very sophisticated. I remember a time when this one wouldn't eat anything he couldn't pronounce."

"I still don't, but I can pronounce more stuff now."

"Hmm." Mrs. Montgomery faced front again, her smile undimmed. "I'd say someone broadened your horizons. Keep at him, Savannah. He's a diamond in the rough."

"Speaking of diamonds," her mom broke in, "I can't wait to see the ring!"

Dang. Her either. Nothing in her jewelry box could pass for an engagement ring. She stared at her naked left hand, and then at Beau. He ran his thumb over her ring finger and gave her an almost imperceptible headshake. Message received. He had nothing.

Stick to the truth as much as possible. Savannah cleared her throat and leaped into the void. "Well, actually, the thing about the ring is…I guess I talk about Sinclair's talents a lot, because Beau knew when it came to something as important as the rings we'd use to symbolize our love, I'd want her to design them. We planned to ask her today after we made our big announcement."

Their moms sighed in unison, but she battled a stab of regret. Her sister designed and created gorgeous, distinctive, and increasingly coveted jewelry, and Savannah had secretly dreamed of someday asking Sinclair to design her rings, but now she'd wasted the once-in-a-lifetime special gesture on this sham engagement. When she finally found the right man to spend the rest of her life with, how could she go to her sister and ask her to design the "perfect rings" for her again? On the other hand, if Mitch had gotten down on his cheating knee last night and proposed, he probably would have presented her with a standard platinum-and-diamond solitaire of whatever color, cut, clarity, and carat befitted the spouse of a junior partner at Cromwell & Cox. He would have wanted the same when it came to the wedding rings, because why spend money on an outward show of sentiment if it didn't also convey a definitive message about his taste, status, and money?

She'd dodged a Tiffany & Co. bullet when she got right down to it, and from here on out she should take a page from Beau's playbook—specifically the "not worry about the future" page. Hell, maybe there was no right man for her? She ought to enjoy this fake engagement to the utmost, because it could be the closest she came to fulfilling the silly wedding fantasies she carted around in her mental hope chest.

Her mom steered the Navigator into a guest spot near the entrance to the complex and the dads pulled into the open slot beside them. "Any thoughts on a dress yet? I know you don't consider yourself a traditional girl, but you look nice in white."

"I don't know, Mom." Strapless white mermaid dress. Hair swept up, no veil, and the tallest heels she could find.

Beau held the door for her, helped her out of the car, and kept her hand clasped in his. Goodness, she'd never had such an attentive fiancé.

"If you're planning a spring wedding, you've got plenty of time to shop," Mrs. Montgomery pointed out as they made their way upstairs.

"But if you want to move more quickly…"

"Jesus, Mom—"

"What? Oops. That came out wrong. I'm not saying you *need* to move more quickly. Um…do you?"

"Should I get my shotgun?" her father joked, sending her a wink.

"Only if you want me to use it on Mom."

They stopped in front of her door. Beau raised their joined hands to his mouth and kissed her wrist. "We haven't talked about timing yet, but there's no particular rush."

The first touch of his lips to her skin since they were babies sent a current of heat straight up her arm. Yes, he could muster up a convincing public display of affection. Too convincing. A thousand new ideas about her fantasy wedding ran through her mind…all of them involving the wedding night and those lips of his roving over her entire body.

The door swung open. "Oh my God, you two. Get a room." Sinclair fanned her face.

Beau nudged her inside, and the sarcastic retort on the tip of her tongue evaporated as she took in the dining table, complete with seven settings and two extra chairs she suspected Sinclair had lugged over from Beau's apartment. The handblown champagne flutes she'd made years ago sparkled against the Irish lace tablecloth Grandma Smith had given her when she left home for college. She'd used it precisely once, and couldn't even guess which drawer or cabinet Sinclair had dug it out of. The drop cloth from her bedroom had been folded into a rectangular banner and now hung across the kitchen archway, with bold yellow letters painted across the front, reading "Congratulations!"

"Wow. The place looks amazing. I can't believe you went to all this trouble."

She shrugged. "I had time to kill, and I wanted today to be special, despite not going as planned."

Salt stung the backs of her eyes. She laid the blame for her hyperemotional state on a sleepless night, her not-gone-as-planned life, and plain, old-fashioned guilt. Sinclair had invested considerable effort on account of a lie.

What if there is no such thing as a harmless deception?

Oh God. She couldn't do this.

Chapter Six

Savannah wore her emotions the same way she wore her clingy black thermals — as if she had nothing to hide. Fine and dandy, when it came to the shirt and leggings, not so fine when it came to the panic Beau read clear as day in her eyes.

"Thanks, Sinclair. Today is special, no matter what happens." He dropped a hand to the nape of Savannah's neck and gently squeezed the muscles knotted there. They relaxed infinitesimally under his touch, and she exhaled slowly.

He understood her second thoughts. Honestly, he did. The conversation during the drive home, the celebratory homecoming Sinclair arranged, all took their deception out of the hypothetical. Shit had gotten real, and now they both realized pulling this off involved a big lie supported by a hundred little ones. While the end, for him, justified the means, it might not for her. They were his parents, after all, not hers, and she would have a harder time reconciling her desire to ease their minds with her discomfort over deceiving her loved ones.

As much as he wanted to pull her aside and give her a pep

talk, she deserved some time alone to run the reconciliation for herself. Normally, an apartment full of family precluded significant alone time, but he could buy her twenty minutes or so, depending on how fast she scrubbed.

"Will anyone starve if I grab a shower before dinner?"

"Goodness no," Mrs. Smith said. "I'm sure both of you would like to clean up."

Sinclair marched over to the fridge, grabbed a bottle of champagne from inside, and held it up. "We'll be fine."

"Okay. Great. I'll be back in a few." He turned to head over to his apartment, but caught his mom watching him expectantly. And Savannah's mom. And Sinclair. *What?* Then he looked at Savannah, and her words from earlier came back to him.

Our families might expect an occasional display of affection.

Apparently so. He wrapped an arm around her waist, pulled her in close, and lowered his head to give her a kiss. She tipped her face up and puckered her lips for a quick, affectionate peck. Perfect. That's all they needed. His lips brushed hers, and…

The velvety cushion gave under the pressure of his mouth. And gave. And kept on giving. His brain shouted, *Abort!* but his lips disregarded the order and went back for more while the rest of his body enjoyed a surge of desire more powerful than he'd experienced in a long time. A very long time. Too long.

Those soft lips opened for his tongue, and her fingers curled into the front of his shirt. Other parts of him went rogue, and the next thing he knew, he had a handful of her sweet, round ass. Her quick intake of breath shot another hot bolt of lust through him. He tightened his grip. She grasped his shoulders and came up on her tiptoes, and he imagined the scrape of her nipples over his chest through the layers of clothes. He plunged his fingers into her hair and pulled her even closer, took the kiss deeper…

Montgomery, you are fucked.

"Don't mind me. I'm just gonna stick my head in the freezer for a second."

Sinclair's comment pierced the fog of need obliterating his self-control. He pulled back, as did Savannah. They both dropped their hands and stepped away from each other, which only made the moment more awkward. Awkward for everyone, judging by the sound of his father clearing his throat. So much for a casual farewell. There was nothing quick or affectionate about the kiss, and the intensity of the attraction might well work against him, because Savannah looked downright shell-shocked. He probably looked the same.

No means of silently reassuring her they could stick to the plan sprang to mind, so he went with retreat and turned to leave. And nearly barreled into his mom. She hugged him, and he inhaled the familiar scent of Chanel No. 5.

"Even with a trip to the emergency room, this easily ranks as the best Thanksgiving ever. For the first time in too long, we feel truly thankful."

He hugged her back and glanced over his shoulder at Savannah. She sent him a weak smile.

"I'm glad," he murmured, broke eye contact to kiss his mom's cheek, and hoped for the best as he walked across the hall.

He showered in surprisingly little time—gotta love water-based paint—and changed into the one pair of black dress pants in his closet and a light gray cashmere sweater his mom had bought him somewhere along the line. A sarcastic voice in the back of his head asked him if he seriously believed pants and a sweater competed with Brooks Brothers. He told the voice to shut the fuck up.

A short call to work sorted out the schedule for tomorrow. He'd come in and do desk stuff if he felt up to it. With that loose end tied off, he made his way back to Savannah's apartment and slipped inside to figure out if any true confessions had occurred during his absence.

Both sets of parents, and Sinclair, sat around the coffee table. Next to the bowl sat an uncorked bottle of champagne in a silver ice bucket. At least one round of toasts had been made by the looks of things, and he took it as a sign he was still engaged. Sinclair and the moms sipped champagne on the sofa. The dads occupied the armchairs, their attention riveted on a bowl game, but their eyes lit up when he moved deeper into the room and they spied the sixer of SweetWater he carried. His dad rose to relieve him of two bottles.

All of this registered in the periphery, though, because Savannah walked in from the kitchen and claimed his attention. She must have put her hair up when she'd showered. It cascaded over her shoulders, with just a few damp tendrils gleaming in the light from the dining room fixture. She leaned over and placed a gravy boat on the table. The neckline of her black sweater gaped, and he caught a wisp of black lingerie before she straightened and absently adjusted the top. Was she wearing the same bra she'd had on before? Hard to say, but a picture of her pale, generous breasts encased in the black lace flashed through his memory, and now he had some adjusting to do.

He took care of it as discreetly as possible while putting the beer in her fridge. Behind him, Savannah announced, "Dinner is served."

Everyone flowed into the dining area and took seats around the table. He sat opposite Savannah, with his mom on his left and his dad on his right. They joined hands for silent grace, said amen, and then…holy shit, he should have prayed for mercy because the conversation took a fast, dangerous turn and dragged him along like a tin can tied to a bumper.

Savannah's mom passed the potatoes and said, "We should shop for dresses when you come home for the Daughters of Magnolia Grove Christmas Eve dinner."

His parents turned to him in unison. "You're coming home for Christmas Eve?" His mom asked the question cautiously. Hopefully.

Hell, no. The last time he'd come home for Christmas Eve, Kelli had been pregnant. Life had seemed so bright and shiny and full of blessings. Less than a year later fate had snatched all those blessings away. He'd skipped the occasion—and the painful memories of what should have been—ever since.

"I don't—"

"We wouldn't miss it," Savannah interrupted, and gave him an impatient look. One that said, *You're doing this to make them happy, so make them happy already.*

Fuck. He hadn't requested the time off. He'd be swapping shifts and owing favors to God and everyone just to clear his schedule.

"We'll have to ride our contractor to get the basement done in time," his dad said to his mom, and shot him a grin. "You and Savannah will be the first to try out our guest suite."

There you go, Smith. Want to bite back the "We wouldn't miss it"?

She chugged her champagne, swallowed with an audible gulp, and said, "Guest suite?"

"Oh, yes," his mom chimed in, nodding. "It will be very comfortable. King bed, fireplace, fancy bathroom. There's even a small, separate sitting room."

"That is so sweet of you, but I wouldn't want to impose, or make anyone uncomfortable," Savannah said.

"Oh please." Her mom dismissed the comment with a wave of her hand. "You're full-grown adults, you're engaged, and you practically live together as it is." She pointed in the general direction of Beau's apartment across the hall. "Besides, if you're in the Montgomerys' basement, that leaves our spare room available for Sinclair."

"Hey now"—Sinclair froze with her fork halfway to her mouth—"I have a perfectly good place of my own."

"Honey, I refuse to leave you holed up in that barn you call home over the holidays. You'll spend Christmas with us. Your sister and Beau will stay with the Montgomerys. It's settled."

"Sounds"—Savannah swallowed again, and her lips drifted into the off-center smile—"lovely."

"After Christmas, I'll set up meetings and tours at the country club, Lakeview Landing, and the Oglethorpe Inn," her mother continued, then looked at Beau's mom. "Anywhere else, Cheryl?"

"Maybe the Whitehall Plantation?"

Mrs. Smith pointed a finger at his mom. "Absolutely." Her finger shifted to him and Savannah. "You two should see what these places have to offer as possible wedding venues."

Were the walls closing in? Suddenly he was spending Christmas in Magnolia Grove, sharing a bed with a woman he'd just promised himself he wouldn't complicate things with, and touring half the county for potential wedding sites. Hell, he might even have to plunk down a nonrefundable deposit to make the charade look real. When he'd thought about a hundred little lies, he hadn't anticipated taking their show on the road and putting on an act for his entire hometown. The lidocaine from the stitches started to wear off, and his head ached like a son of a bitch.

But he took in the sight of his parents leaning toward each other, strategizing about how to get the basement done in time, and where to put the tree, and he felt the tightness in his chest abate. They glowed with anticipation. All he had to do was stay the course and he'd give them the merriest

Christmas they'd had in a long time. They deserved it.

So he plastered a smile on his face, fielded questions as best he could, and nodded with Savannah when his parents mentioned they'd be back in Atlanta the following week for an appointment with a specialist and wanted to take their son and future daughter-in-law out for dinner. At the end of the evening he congratulated himself when both sets of family huddled for a last round of hugs before meandering down the hall, leaving a trail of chatter behind them.

"Drive safe," Savannah called, and shut the door. Then she sagged against it, expelled a breath, and rubbed her hands over her face in a gesture he already recognized signaled fatigue.

"Thank you." His quiet words seemed to fill the apartment.

She straightened and smiled up at him. "You're welcome. All in all, I thought it went pretty well."

"You did amazing. My parents are high-fiving each other right now."

"I'd say both sets of parents are high-fiving right now. I'm almost offended." She moved away from the door. "I had no idea I was such a lost cause."

"You're the catch. I'm the lost cause."

Her eyes roamed his face for a long moment. Finally, she said, "Nobody's caught and nobody's lost. We're both works in progress."

Her fingertips skimmed along the front of his hair. She was a toucher, he'd already noticed, and anything textured drew her—the flannel shirt he'd worn to the hospital, his sweater, his hair. As an artist, the tactile tendency probably came with the territory, but he'd have to get used to it or spend the next few weeks dealing with a constant hard-on.

"How's your head?"

Let me pull it out of my pants and check. It felt like someone had taken a hammer to his frontal bone, but he said,

"Fine."

"Sure it is. And your eye always twitches in time to the invisible drummer banging on your skull." She strolled into the kitchen, opened a cabinet, and pulled out an industrial-sized bottle of ibuprofen. "How many would you like?"

So much for his tough-guy stoicism. "Three hundred."

She laughed, tipped three tablets into her palm, and handed them to him, along with his glass of water from dinner.

He downed the pills while Savannah yawned so big he could have examined her tonsils if she hadn't brought her fist up to block her mouth. "Tired?"

"I guess I am." She leaned against the kitchen counter and glanced at the clock on her stove. "God, how pathetic. It's not even nine."

"I'll shove off and let you get some rest. Tomorrow I'll come by, get my chairs, and we can talk. Decide how we play this thing out."

"Wait." She held out her hand, palm up. "I need a key so I can wake you up later and make sure your brain isn't swelling." With her other hand, she unconsciously smoothed her sweater over her hips.

Something was swelling, but not his brain. "You're tired. Get some sleep. I'll be fine."

"Uh-uh. *I* won't be fine. Dr. West gave me very specific instructions and I'll lose sleep worrying about you if I don't follow them to the letter. Name, birthday, and finger count, once at eleven and again at three. Two check-ins mandatory and a third at seven recommended. I've already set my alarm."

"I don't remember her using the word 'mandatory.'"

"Are you afraid I'm going to laugh at your jammies or something?"

He spent another useless minute arguing the check-ins weren't necessary, but she pulled out the symptom sheet she'd gotten at the hospital, ticked off headache, irritability, and memory loss, and suggested maybe she should go ahead and call an ambulance. He relented, retrieved his extra key, and handed it over with an exasperated, "See you at eleven. For the record, I sleep naked."

"For the record, I've already seen you naked," she tossed back, just before she closed the door.

Very funny. Sharing a bath as infants hardly qualified as seeing him naked. Even so, he caught himself smiling as he got ready for bed. In deference to his night nanny, he left the hall light burning, and pulled on an old pair of sweatpants and a not-so-old white T-shirt before he crawled into bed. He picked up the remote from his nightstand and turned on the TV centered on the wall across from his bed. With the sound down, he clicked over to the sports network, thinking he'd catch some final scores, but then found himself listening to Savannah humming to herself through the wall. It took him a moment to place the song.

"Before He Cheats." Yeah, this is where he'd come in.

When she got to the "pretty little souped-up four-wheel drive" part she broke off. A moment later her bedsprings squeaked and a light knock came from the wall behind his head, followed by a muffled, "Night, Beau."

"Night, Savannah," he replied, and tried to concentrate on the TV rather than every little squeak and groan of her mattress as she shifted around for a comfy position. His imagination offered up a graphic slide show of possible positions for her to assume.

He focused on the scores scrolling across the crawl at the bottom of the screen. North Carolina beat Duke. Good. Penn State beat Wisconsin. The Bruins beat the Trojans *and* covered the spread. Miracle. The network cut to a commercial and he rested his eyes for a second…

Savannah's scent surrounded him. Her breath fanned his cheek as she whispered his name. One busy hand drifted over his shoulder and down his chest. His subconscious mind hadn't treated him to a dream this vivid in a long time, but his body rushed to enjoy it. "Lower," he murmured. She shifted and said his name again, a little louder this time.

She liked loud. He wanted her loud. The creak of his mattress reminded him she also wanted a comfortable position. No problem. He could scratch that itch. He rolled, pulling her onto the bed, not stopping until he had her sprawled all over him, anticipating the slide of skin on skin.

Inexplicable layers of clothes and sheets thwarted the skin-on-skin goal, but the warm weight of her breasts rested against his chest. Her slender thighs straddled his waist, and incredibly soft, incredibly hot flesh kissed his abdomen. She wiggled backward—he couldn't fathom why—but the move brought the yielding curves of her ass into contact with the straining head of his cock. He groaned his approval, and centered them up a bit.

"Beau." Even louder now, and slightly breathless.

He tightened his abs, flattened his hand against the small of her back, and pressed her closer.

"Oh, jeez. Beau."

Toes curled into calves. He slid his free hand up the back of her thigh, raising fabric as he went.

"Beau!"

Chapter Seven

Thanks to the glow of the hall light and the flicker of the TV, Savannah knew the minute Beau woke up. She saw his eyes open, focus on her, and then watched awareness creep into his sleep-dazed face as he took stock of their situation. He had her draped over him with her fleece robe tangled around her legs, one hand splayed across her hips, and the other clamped to her lower back, his rugged abs providing a perfect saddle for a long, hard, and very dirty ride.

A not-so-subtle nudge around back announced at least one part of him was wide awake. Fully. Awake.

He stared at her mouth for what seemed like forever, not moving a muscle, and she stared right back, remembering the power of his kiss—the explosive heat unleashed by the simple contact of lips to lips. Their "no complications" rule was already bent all to hell. If he kissed her right now, it would be completely and irreparably broken. Even knowing this, she couldn't say whether she hoped he'd pull her closer or ease her away.

The white gauze taped to his forehead caught her attention

and made up her mind for her. His injury. The whole reason she was here in the first place. She propped her forearm on his chest and made the peace sign. "How many fingers am I holding up?"

He lowered his chin a degree and looked down at her hand. "I'm usually the one asking that question."

"Let's hope you can also answer."

"Let's hope."

Two fingertips traced a meandering pattern down her back all the way to the base of her spine. She shivered, but stayed strong. "I'm afraid I have to insist on a verbal response."

"Two," he said, and shifted his hips, managing to dislodge his personal parts from hers in the process. "Do I owe you an apology?"

He couldn't have looked or sounded less apologetic, with his shadowed jaw, growly voice, and general air of tense, dissatisfied male. She held back a grin.

"No need. After all, we're engaged." She crawled off him and settled onto her back on the bed, then double-checked her robe to make sure all the essentials remained covered. They both stared at the ceiling and took a moment to settle.

"Ready to play doctor?"

She felt rather than saw him turn his head to look at her. "Only if I get to be the doctor."

The grin threatened again, but she shook her head. "Maybe next time. What's your name?"

"This seems like something my fiancée would know."

"I'm not asking for me, I'm asking for you."

"I already know my name."

She thumped him on the leg with the back of her hand. "Don't make me beat it out of you. Dr. West told me to have you recite your name and date of birth."

"Ow. I liked your earlier bedside manner better. My name is Beauregard Miller Montgomery."

"Beauregard?" Now she turned to look at him. He had his arm propped behind his head and stared at the ceiling again. Nice profile. "How did I not know Beau was short for Beauregard?"

"It's my paternal grandmother's maiden name. There's a way-back connection to General P.T.G. Beauregard."

"Impressive. And Miller?"

"My mom's maiden name. Now you know as much as I do."

Strangely, she did feel a bit more intimately acquainted, though the conversation might not be the sole cause. "I'm prepared for the fiancée quiz."

"If there's going to be a quiz, we better exchange this information, don't you think?"

"Wait. I'm not done with my questions yet. I need your date of birth."

"August sixth."

"Hmm. That's a problem."

"You got something against Leos?"

"Not at all. But assuming we started dating shortly after I moved into Camden Gardens, and now we're engaged, I surely gave you a birthday gift reflective of my deep and abiding love. A keepsake."

"You did?"

"Of course I did. I'm a romantic soul. I gave you something thoughtful, and fun. Something you'd treasure forever."

"You gave me a Ducati?"

"You really are suffering a brain injury if you think I can afford a Duc. I'm a starving artist. No. I gave you"—she tried to imagine a personal gift she could actually afford—"an original glass sculpture of my own design. You keep it on your coffee table, so you can show it off when people visit."

He looked worried. "A small, unobtrusive sculpture?"

Okay, she wouldn't take the comment personally. The

man kept no mementos of any kind in his apartment, and her "gift" threatened to disrupt the sterile, uncluttered surfaces of his home. "Very small," she assured him. "I know my man. But we need to make a few changes, because right now, this place doesn't bear the stamp of guy in a serious relationship. No pictures of us at a Braves game, no seashells picked from the surf during a long weekend in Pismo Beach. Nada."

The rasp of a hard palm across whiskers filled the silence, and every delicate expanse of skin on her body clamored to be on the receiving end of the subtle abrasion. Not wise. He was, though, and she read him well enough to know he saw her point.

"Don't go to a lot of trouble. My parents don't come to my place."

"They're coming next week, and we want to make this look real. It's no trouble. It's not like I'm under the gun creating new works for a big exhibit anywhere."

As soon as the words left her lips, she wanted to bite them back. *He already knows the pathetic state of your personal life, and now you want to parade your professional failure in front of him?* Maybe he hadn't noticed the self-directed sarcasm in her voice.

"Did the glass art market take a downturn?"

Nope. He heard. She pressed the heel of her hand to the place above her eye where a headache tried to take root. "It did for me."

"I have no idea how the art world works. Did you get a bad review or a lousy write-up or something?"

"No, nothing like that." Though taste was subjective, and negative opinions came with the territory. Those she could handle. "I climbed into bed with the wrong people. And despite how that sounds, it's a boring story. Forget I said anything."

The mattress gave as he rolled onto his side to face her.

"It's on your mind. Seems like the kind of thing your fiancé would know about. Maybe I can help?" He found the ache over her eyebrow, and ironed the sore spot with his thumb.

Paramedic by trade, rescuer by nature. She'd best remember that. "You're sweet, but there's nothing you can do. Oh, hey, look at the time. I should go. I'm supposed to wake you up, not keep you up."

A warm hand curled around her forearm when she started to move.

"How am I supposed to pass the fiancé quiz if I don't know about your career? C'mon, Smith. Spill."

Shoot. Trapped by her own argument. And yeah, a real fiancé probably would know her first effort to make a name for herself in a regional market had failed miserably. If not for the fellowship, she'd been at serious risk of celebrating her twenty-eighth birthday by moving back in with her parents.

"Okay. Fine." She flopped onto her side, facing him. "Here's the deal. Earlier this year a hot new gallery in Atlanta offered to represent me."

He folded an arm behind his head and turned to look at her. "Congratulations. Is that what brought you here?"

"Yep. The gallery owners suggested I move closer so I could support their marketing investment by attending showings, doing client meet-and-greets, and generally circulating in the local art scene."

"Sounds logical, I guess."

"I thought so. I'd done well in Athens, but the scene there is only so big, and mostly supported by my school. After undergrad and my MFA, I felt like I'd wrung all I could out of Lamar Dodd."

"Time to stop being the big fish in a pond?"

"Exactly. Moving represented the next logical step in my growth, and I arrived with a smile on my face and stars in my eyes, but not enough hard information about my new business representatives." She fiddled with the sheet, folding a corner into the world's smallest accordion. "I ignored rumors about financial problems, and some not-so-legit deals. A couple months ago the owners got busted for selling forged Warhols on eBay, and the gallery shut its doors soon after."

"That sucks. Can you get your work back and jump to another gallery?"

"Unfortunately it's not that easy. They sold five of my pieces—presumably collected payment in full—but only paid me partial commissions for two. In theory, I can sue them for what they owe me, but Mit...um...my legal adviser said he didn't see the Feds unfreezing their assets to pay my judgment while the mail and wire fraud charges drag on. Meanwhile, despite marketing myself like crazy to other reputable galleries, no one's calling."

"Screw 'em." He stared at the ceiling again, a slight furrow in his brow. "Represent yourself. Get a good photographer and a web designer and open your own virtual showroom online. Who needs a gallery?"

She appreciated the show of support, but she knew better. "I do. In part because nobody knows who I am, so I need a gallery to publicize me and present me to potential collectors, and in part because my works are three-dimensional and respond to nuances of light and shadow. People need to view them in person to get the full impact."

"I can't drive a block around this city without running into an art festival or street fair—"

"And there's nothing wrong with art festivals and street fairs, but many of my pieces are large, and all of them are breakable." He was picturing embedded flower paperweights and Murano vases. She did six-foot waves of indigo glass curling into millefiori foams of silver, cobalt, and sapphire. Her vases came complete with cascading glass blossoms dripping with prisms of dew, attracting enough breathtakingly fragile glass bees and butterflies to make a Dutch master weep. "I can't cart them around to every art festival in Atlanta. Even if the breakage risk didn't deter me, my price point makes those venues a waste of time."

His eyes cut back to her. "What's your price point?"

"If you have to ask…"

"And yet you're broke."

"Because I haven't gotten paid. Those slick-bellied sons of guns owe me over forty thousand in commissions, but I can't devalue my name because of my current circumstances. If I started churning out twenty-dollar paperweights and fifty-dollar vases to sell at coffee shops and farmers' markets, I might as well kiss my fine-art prospects good-bye."

"What about your pen pals at the Solomon Foundation? Do they have a gallery?"

"The Solomon Foundation has everything." She closed her eyes and imagined the palazzo on the Grand Canal. "Museums throughout the world, a network of galleries and collectors, plus patronage. They offer fellowships to selected artists. The foundation provides fellows with studio space and living quarters to enable them to pursue their projects."

"You should apply for one of those fellowships."

"I did, actually. The week I learned I'd been hosed by my gallery I kind of panicked and sent out applications and proposals to a bunch of different programs. Hence the letter you received by mistake."

"And…?"

The prompt made her smile. She opened her eyes and winked at him. "They offered me a nine-month fellowship starting in January."

"Congratulations." The sincerity in his voice quickly shifted to curiosity. "Why didn't you say something earlier? You could have celebrated the news with your family."

"What? And steal the spotlight away from our big

announcement?"

"We could have celebrated both."

She let go of the sheet and snugged into his "guest" pillow. Her eyelids weighed a thousand pounds. She had to leave soon, or she'd fall asleep in his bed. "The two pieces of news don't really mesh all that well."

"How so? I'm all for your career."

"Hmm. The fellowship is in Venice."

The mattress shifted as he raised his head. "Venice, Italy?"

"Uh-huh. I'm afraid my career opportunity comes at the expense of my relationship."

He settled back against his pillow. "Huh. I can't believe you're choosing Venice over us."

"It's the chance of a lifetime. If you really loved me, you'd support my decision." *Yeah, like Mitch.* He'd encouraged her to apply, mentioned the firm had offices in Rome and how he could visit often and steal her away for weekends in Paris. And keep her at arm's length the rest of the time, while he planned his wedding to another woman.

"This works, you know."

"Yeah. I figure we make the announcement in between Christmas and New Year's, and explain to our families we're postponing the wedding until I return. Then during the time apart we realize we're not meant to be. We break up. An Italian prince sweeps me off my feet, we have half a dozen bambinos, and live happily ever after."

"I think they dismantled the Italian monarchy after World War II, but I have no doubt the men of Italy will line up to sweep you off your feet and make you happy."

"Easy for you to say." But then again, maybe it wasn't. She detected a hint of something cautious beneath the humor. He didn't believe in happily ever after. She wished she could see his face, but it was too much trouble to open her eyes.

"Are you falling asleep on me?"

"I'm awake."

"Okay. So answer me this. What did I get you for your birthday?"

She frowned into the darkness. "Nothing. We didn't know each other yet...or again...whatever."

"We didn't?" His rumbly voice sounded a little soft around the edges.

"No. I moved here in April. My birthday is February fourteenth."

"Valentine's Day?" His finger traced her upper lip. "How's that working out for you?"

Hearts and flowers mixed with cake and presents? Could be worse. But she had a hard time finding her vocal cords to reply. Instead she rested her head against his shoulder, enjoying the combination of fresh-washed T-shirt and his scent. A random thought skipped through her mind. "You lied to me."

"Huh?"

"You don't sleep in the nude."

"I dressed up for you." He flexed his shoulder to scoot her head into a more comfortable position. "You do."

She ran her hand along the collar of her robe. "I dressed up for you."

"Savannah?"

Her name sounded sexy in his low, lazy voice. "What?"

"No need to dress up on my account."

Chapter Eight

Beau's feet were freezing, but the rest of him sweated under a strangely heavy fleece blanket. A way-too-warm fleece blanket. Apparently the blanket agreed, because it wiggled, and shifted, and then grew a leg and kneed him in the balls hard enough to make him grunt—and wake up.

A mass of blonde hair greeted his bleary eyes, and beneath the wayward strands he saw Savannah's sleeping face. Dark blonde lashes didn't so much as flutter. The imprint from the edge of the pillowcase creased one cheek. She had his blue comforter wrapped around her like a cocoon, with one smooth, slim leg kicked free and slung across his waist.

His abused balls immediately forgave her, and now he sweated for entirely different reasons. Reasons like imagining sliding his hand along her thigh, easing her onto her back and unwrapping her from the layers of blanket, sheets, and robe until he reached the warm flesh beneath. Waking her slowly—and then quickly—until she tangled her fingers in his hair and screamed loud enough to let everyone in the entire building know she was having a good morning.

Bad idea. They'd both agreed not to act on the attraction. Best to remove himself from temptation, because every second he remained here with her he got a little dumber. He slid out of bed as stealthily as possible and turned off his alarm. Whatever plans she had this morning, he doubted they required her to wake up at six. She snuggled into the warm spot left by his body and mumbled something that sounded a lot like, "Gotta check the pie."

Sweet dreams, Savannah.

He started his shower with a blast of frigid water, which took care of the lingering disagreement between his dick and his brain. After dressing for work, he headed to the kitchen and filled his commuter mug. Then he took a ceramic mug from the cabinet for his guest, but noticed the one sitting behind it and grabbed that one instead. It suited the occasion better. A brief rummage through his junk drawer turned up a notepad and pen. He scribbled a message to his fiancée and left both note and coffee on the nightstand next to sleeping beauty, who had managed to kick off all the covers and most of her robe in the time he'd been gone. She lay facedown across his bed, with one of nature's best works of art on full display. Two shallow dimples guarded a perfect heart-shaped ass. For a pulse-pounding moment he imagined leaning over her, bracketing the spectacular sight, and rousing her with the kind of kiss destined to leave a mark on her and make him late for work. He could practically hear her moan his name in a sleep-husky voice, and feel her arch up, lift her hips to offer him—

A slap in the face, at worst, and a whole lot of complications, at best. Get moving, Montgomery. The only thing you're riding today is a desk.

A half hour later he stood in the break room, pouring his second cup of coffee when his partner, Hunter, wandered in. The rangy blond propped his hip against the counter, sipped his coffee, and smirked. "So, Humpty Dumpty, do anything exciting for Thanksgiving?"

Beau deliberately took his time topping off his mug and setting the carafe back on the warming plate. He waited until his partner had a mouthful of coffee before saying, "Got engaged."

Hunter choked, and then erupted into coughs. "Holy shit. I did not see that coming."

"Me either."

Hunter pulled a small flashlight from his chest pocket and shined the beam into Beau's eye. "Exactly how hard did you get hit in the head?"

He jerked his head away. "Cut it out. My brain's functioning just fine. In fact, I had a flash of genius." To prove it, he laid out the pertinent points of his so-called engagement.

"Holy shit," Hunter repeated at the end of the explanation. "You're temporarily in bed with the tasty little blonde across the hall?"

"We're not 'in bed,' blockhead." But they had been, last night, and waking up next to her had felt better than he cared to admit.

"Hunter Knox, I'm not your maid, and I'm not cleaning the rig all by myself," an exasperated female voice interrupted. "Fetch your coffee, kiss your work-wife good-bye, and get your ass out to the garage."

Beau glanced past his partner to an irate brunette who managed to look like a Hollywood version of a paramedic despite the standard-issue white shirt and dark blue utility pants. "Hey, Ashley."

The shift supervisor's flashing gray eyes switched to him and grew a little less irate. "Hi, Beau. How's the head?"

"Still attached."

"Try to keep it that way. The fewer calls I have to ride out on with the deadweight you call a partner, the better off the greater Atlanta area will be."

"Pardon me for taking an extra minute, whip-cracker. My partner just told me he got engaged."

"Oh, wow. Congratulations." She crossed the room and gave him a hug. "I'm really happy for you."

Over her shoulder he sent Hunter a glare he hoped conveyed his utter *What the fuck?* But his so-called partner refused to look him in the face. Ashley drew away, and Beau dredged up a smile for her. "Thanks."

"I'll want all the details later." She took a step back. "And you have to bring her to the holiday party and introduce her." Her attention clicked to Hunter, and her smile disappeared. "If you're not out helping me clean the truck in three minutes, I'm going to back it over you." With the threat hanging in the air, she turned on her heel and walked out.

As soon as she left, Beau punched his partner hard in the chest. "What the hell were you thinking?"

"Ow." Hunter punched him back. "Nothing. I wanted her to know why I got distracted. You're the one pretending to be engaged. I'm just making it look real."

"I'm pretending to be engaged to my parents, and Savannah's family. Not my coworkers. Not every ER doctor, nurse, and orderly in Atlanta."

"So what if they think you're engaged? Where's the harm? It's not like you're dating anyone else, or almost dating anyone, or contemplating dating anyone."

"But now I have to ask Savannah to come to the holiday party or everyone here will assume I think she's too good for them. And when we *break up*, I'll be the poor sap who couldn't close the deal. No offense, but I've had enough sympathy for a lifetime."

"Okay, fine. Sorry I didn't think it through that far."

"No, you were too busy trying to talk your way off Ashley's shit list. It's a lost cause."

"I don't know why." Hunter picked up a stray napkin from the counter, crumpled it, and hurled it into the trash. "She treats everyone else around here like a professional, but with me, she's all, 'Get your lazy ass out to the garage and don't hand me any excuses.' I'm a nice guy. People like me — especially female people."

"Could be you're trying too hard. She smells the desperation on you."

"What desperation? Normal women find me charming, dammit. I've got plenty of *friends* who can testify to my charm."

"That looks a whole lot more desperate than you realize, Hunt."

"Says the engaged virgin."

"I'm no virgin."

"You might as well be, for all you've used it lately."

A memory of half-naked Savannah in his bed spun through his mind, taunting him more than anything his partner said. He held up a hand to reject all of it — the flashback, the powerful longing, the entire conversation. "I've used it." One-night stands counted, and while he didn't hook up often, he hadn't taken a vow of chastity.

"Not in a meaningful way," Hunter argued.

True. He avoided meaningful, unless one considered a few sweaty hours of strictly physical release with a like-minded partner meaningful. Even as the thought formed in his head, the image of Savannah stubbornly resurfaced. Time to shift the focus of this discussion away from him. "Your definition of meaningful involves having 'plenty of friends.' I think it's safe to assume Ash doesn't find the whole man-whore thing endearing."

"Why should she care? She's engaged to some jarhead — God help him — and I have a few morals about that kind of thing, anyway. All I'm asking is for a little respect."

"I think you're SOL, Aretha. Maybe you remind her of an ex, or something."

"So I get my ass kicked just for showing up? How is that fair?"

"Why am I still waiting, Knox?" The question sailed into the break room from down the hall. Ashley's patience had expired.

"Life's not fair, Hunt."

Hunter finished the last swallow of his coffee and banged the mug down on the counter. He tossed Beau a cocky smile. "I love a challenge."

Beau waved at his partner's back and tried hard not to laugh. Then he prayed for Atlanta, because Hunter and Ashley wouldn't survive twelve hours together in the rig.

• • •

Savannah inhaled sheets that smelled like Tide, and the scent immediately transported her to her formative years. Were it not for the underlying notes of aftershave and testosterone, she might have believed she lolled in her childhood bed. But the havoc those additional scents wreaked on her system was anything but childish.

She cracked an eye open and stared around an unfamiliar bedroom. Well, not totally unfamiliar. It featured the same basic shape, size, and layout as hers, and served the same basic purpose, but otherwise, this stark, clutter-free blank canvas couldn't have been more different.

Beau's bedroom. Whoops, she'd fallen asleep here after all. But where was the man of the house? She looked around the empty room. Her meandering gaze landed on the folded note propped against a coffee mug. She levered herself up on her arms, and—yikes. Her robe was tangled around her waist. When had that happened? Hopefully after Beau had left the room. A couple tugs righted the situation, and then she crawled over to the nightstand. The smell of coffee beckoned. Black, just like she preferred. She picked up the mug, took a taste, and paused to savor the brew. Not bad. Only after she swallowed did she notice the printing on the mug.

Feel safe at night. Sleep with an EMT.

She laughed. Mission accomplished, and she did feel safe. But alone. Something about the quiet apartment told her she had the place to herself. The note sat on the nightstand like a tiny paper tent. She opened it and found a few lines of strong, spare script written across the page.

> *Thanks for checking on me last night.*
> *Later,*
> *Beau*
> *P.S. Nice pjs.*

Whoops, again. The only pjs she wore were the ones God had given her, and apparently she'd modeled them for Beau this morning. Falling asleep in nothing but a bathrobe certainly courted the risk, but she hadn't counted on spending the night when she'd tossed the thing on to run across the hall and give him a vision test and memory quiz. Lord knew he'd handled more than his fair share of Savannah Smith T&A in the last twenty-four hours, but the thought of him looking his fill at some of the package while she slept left her a teensy bit embarrassed—and a lot turned on. She fanned her face with the note, and then, for some reason she couldn't explain, brought the paper to her face and sniffed, mildly disappointed to find it didn't smell like him. It didn't smell like anything.

The bedside clock read half past seven. She needed to get a move on. Her bedroom wasn't going to finish painting itself, and she'd spent some of her rapidly dwindling savings on discounted studio time at Glassworks this evening, in hopes of completing new pieces by the end of the month—

on the nonexistent chance one of the galleries she'd queried decided to add her to their stable of artists on exhibit in time for Christmas. Now she could add Beau's birthday present to her project list.

Another sip of coffee fortified her enough to get out of bed. The next sip got her moving toward the front door, and convinced her the coffee was too good to leave behind. She'd get the mug back to him later. Besides, if a girl couldn't borrow a mug from her fiancé, the relationship needed work.

The sound of her phone greeted her as soon as she stepped into her apartment. It sat charging on her kitchen counter, and she picked it up to see Sinclair trying to FaceTime her. She hit accept and braced for anything.

Her sister's smiling face filled the little screen—always an enviable sight. Whereas Savannah looked in a mirror and saw her mom's untamable blonde hair, soft features, and curvy but diminutive frame staring back at her, Sinclair appeared to have cherry-picked the best of both parents. She had their dad's thick black hair and tall, lean physique. They shared their mom's eye color, but Sinclair's inky hair intensified ordinary blue into something exotic.

Sinclair also got their dad's dark, arching brows, and she raised one now for full, sardonic effect. "How's one half of the happiest couple south of the Mason-Dixon line this fine morning?"

"I don't know. Which half are you referring to? Mom or Mrs. Montgomery?"

Sinclair laughed, and the same mischievous dimple Savannah remembered sticking her finger in as a kid appeared in her sister's cheek. "Might as well start calling Mrs. Montgomery Mom now, too, don't you think?"

"I'm not calling her Mom unless I can blame her for all my shortcomings."

"Bite your tongue. The beautiful and talented Savannah

Smith has no shortcomings."

"It's too early in the morning to mock me."

"I suppose you can be a tad moody."

"That's Mom's fault." She dropped into one of the chairs around her small dining room table—one of Beau's chairs—and sipped Beau's coffee from Beau's mug. Definitely a theme going this morning.

"And vague—a trait you share with your soon-to-be spouse."

A small knot of guilt twisted tighter in her stomach. "How so?"

"You asked me to design your rings, but neither of you gave me much to go on. I need details. What type of metal? Gemstones or no gemstones? A time frame would be helpful." She held up a sketch pad filled with half a dozen small, intricately wrought designs. "I worked on some preliminary drawings when I got home last night, but I have no idea if I'm on the right track..."

The guilt knot turned into guilt macramé. "You're not. No, that came out wrong. Your sketches are beautiful, but, Sinclair, put your pencil down."

Her sister's frown filled the screen. "What's going on?"

Savannah took a gulp of coffee and hoped the caffeine would kick-start her brain, because she needed to give Sinclair a logical reason to hold off on ring designs. "Umm..."

Sinclair's eyes narrowed. "Yesterday when you guys went to the ER and I stayed back to clean up and tend to dinner, I noticed a few interesting things."

"Interesting?"

"Yeah. For instance, you guys didn't seem to have coordinated the menu at all. I basted two turkeys—either of which would have been sufficient to feed all of us—warmed two different stuffing recipes, and cooked a broccoli cheese casserole *and* a green bean casserole."

"We wanted everyone to have their favorites…"

"Conceivable," Sinclair acknowledged, "but I also cleaned up your bedroom and spent time in both your apartments. Aside from one paint-stained shirt, I didn't find a trace of his stuff in your place. Not a stray sock, or a bottle of beer in the fridge, or an extra toothbrush in the bathroom. And granted, I only spent time in his kitchen, but I didn't see a single thing of yours in his unit, either. One might think you'd never set foot in each other's homes."

"Or we're tidy?"

Sinclair simply shook her head. "You're not tidy."

Okay, apparently her conscience drew fine lines when it came to fabricating. Letting people jump to conclusions was one thing, but she couldn't look her sister in the eye and lie. "You're right. I'm not tidy. I can explain…" And she did, as concisely as possible, covering everything from Mitch's indecent proposal, to Beau's impulsive one, and their prearranged breakup thanks to her fellowship.

"Hole-E-crap," Sinclair said as soon as Savannah stopped talking.

"Don't tell anyone."

"My lips are sealed, but you ought to know Mom practically planned your wedding during the drive back to Magnolia Grove. I think she emailed the *Gazette* an engagement announcement last night."

She bit back a groan. "Now that you know the score, can't you rein her in?"

"You've met our mom, right? Exactly how do you propose I rein her in?"

"I don't know. Have a crisis. Give her something else to focus on."

"Short of setting myself on fire, there's no distracting her from your wedding. She and Cheryl Montgomery are going to have your venue selected and booked before you can say

I don't."

"That's exactly the kind of thing I need you to put a stop to. Don't design rings. Don't book venues. Be busy when she suggests shopping for dresses."

"No amount of tap-dancing on my part will make a difference. You know as well as I our mom is a hundred-and-ten-pound steamroller. If you don't find a way to come clean to her, it won't matter how far across the globe you run. You and Beau are going to end up married through the sheer force of Mom's will."

Chapter Nine

The rap of knuckles on wood reached Beau from halfway down the stairs, along with an exasperated male voice calling, "Savannah, open the door. This is ridiculous. You can't avoid me forever."

He reached the landing to find One-for-Three standing in front of Savannah's door. The guy glanced at Beau, then smoothed a hand over his $200 haircut, straightened his tie, and resumed knocking. "Savannah—"

A primitive urge to grab the smaller man by the back of his double-breasted coat and shove him into the trash chute surged through Beau, but he tamped it down. He'd sworn an oath to conserve life, alleviate suffering, and do no harm. Kicking One-for-Three's unsuspecting ass just for being there probably did not comply with the code. Instead he shifted his grocery bag to one arm, slipped his key into his lock, and said over his shoulder, "She's not home."

"Excuse me?" One-for-Three turned and stared at him.

"Savannah's not home."

The man's baby-smooth forehead creased. "I've been

trying to reach her for days. Where is she?"

She was at the studio, working. They'd been fake-engaged less than a week and he already knew her schedule better than this knob who'd dated her for half a year. He shrugged and opened his door. "If she wanted you to know, you'd know, doncha think?" He pushed his door open and stepped inside.

"Wait!"

Beau placed his grocery bag on the small table inside the door and then faced Savannah's ex and crossed his arms.

"I'm Mitchell Prescott the third, Savannah's…friend. When will she be back?"

Could be five minutes, or five hours, depending on how her work went. "Same answer, friend. If she wanted you to know, you'd know."

"Thanks. You've been a big help."

Maybe the eye roll did the job, or the sarcastic tone, but one way or another this jerkoff managed to light his fuse. Quite an accomplishment, considering he generally had exceptional emotional control. When everyone in the vicinity of a medical emergency lost their shit, people counted on him to stay calm. But tonight one pissy comment had him drawing himself to full height and stepping toward the source of his irritation. "Do you need *more* help?"

One-for-Three's face turned red and his eyes darted left and right. "Relax, buddy…"

He took a step closer and started to say, "I'm not your buddy," but a new set of footsteps on the stairs caught his attention. They both turned to see Savannah come into view. First the tousled bundle of blonde waves, which she'd swept into a recklessly sexy pile on top of her head, then her gorgeous face, decorated by the off-center smile—though she smiled into her big black handbag so neither he nor One-for-Three could take credit for her mood. A dark blue peacoat protected her from the chilly air, and baggy jeans rolled at the ankles covered her legs. Scuffed Doc Martens encased her feet. A reusable shopping bag hung from the crook of her other arm. There was nothing intrinsically sexy about the outfit, but for whatever reason the androgynous clothes only emphasized her femininity. The hum of appreciation he detected from her ex brought on another uncharacteristically violent impulse. His fingers twitched with the compulsion to throttle the man, but he resisted because she looked up just then.

"Hello, Beau." She halted on the landing, and her eyes swung to her ex. Beau braced for her reaction, and told himself his tension stemmed from a reluctance to see her give an inch to this self-indulgent prick. To his relief, her smile disappeared. "Mitch," she said, and dug her keys out of her purse. She placed the shopping bag by her feet. "I knew my day was going too well. To what do I owe this surprise?"

"It should hardly come as a surprise. I left you several messages—"

"To which I didn't respond." She twisted her key in the lock. "My silence should have left *you* a message."

Atta girl. He was about to say something like, "Do you get the fucking message now?" and move Mitch along, when the starched and pressed weasel started laying his heart—or more accurately, a sleazy combination of his pride and his wallet—on the line. "I've missed you. Savannah. I love you, and now that you've had some cooling off time, you must realize there's still a place for you in my life. You're my outlet, my escape. I want to whisk you away for romantic weekends at the Cloisters, or meet up with you at the Ritz in Paris."

Beau waited for her reply, more invested than he wanted to be. Over didn't always mean over. People gave things second, third, fourth tries, and despite their temporary arrangement, he lacked standing to call bullshit on her behalf. They weren't engaged, or even truly involved. He certainly didn't represent her future, and if she sincerely believed this loser might, he couldn't interfere with her poor judgment.

"This may come as a shock to you, Mitch, but I don't give a shit about weekends at the Cloisters or rendezvous at the Paris Ritz. I don't want to be an outlet or escape, or some kind of diversion you pick up and put down at your convenience. The man who earns my heart? He needs to take me on, issues and all. I expect to be his everything—soul mate, partner, friend. And I expect him to be all those things to me. You're clearly not that man. Have a nice life, and stay the hell out of mine."

He put his hand on her arm. "Don't shut me out, baby. We can talk this through."

Savannah looked down at the manicured hand on her arm and then placed her hand over his.

Okay, fuck standing. This situation begged for interference. She'd thank him later. Beau started to reach for lover boy, but Savannah beat him to it. She removed his hand from her arm. "We've said everything we need to say to each other, with the possible exception of this: if you lay a hand on me again, I will clean your clock."

"Baby, please. You know I love you."

The placating tone scraped across Beau's nerves as effectively as nails on a chalkboard. Then the dumbass went in for a kiss. Before Beau could react, Savannah drew her arm back, made a fist, and slammed it into Mitchell Prescott III's pedigreed nose hard enough to snap his head back.

After reaching full extension, his head bounced forward. He leaned over, one hand braced on his knee, the other clutching his blowhole. "Jesus Christ, Savannah, I think—I think you broke my nose!"

"Let's be sure." She shook out her hand and then pulled her fingers into a fist again.

Mitch groaned and straightened. Blood flowed from one

bruised nostril, and the bridge already showed hints of purple.

Apparently the blow left Mitch's eyesight intact. As soon as he saw her poised for round two, he ducked behind Beau. "Call 911."

Beau sighed. "I am 911." He shifted his attention to Savannah, captured her hand, and eyed her abused knuckles. "Nice shot, Champ. Go ice this hand. I'll be over as soon as I get your punching bag squared away."

"I'm fine, and this"—she gestured at Mitch with her uninjured hand—"is not your mess to clean up. If he wants help, he can call his fiancée." She leaned past him to address Mitch, who leaned against Beau's doorframe, pressing a tissue to his nose. "I'd love to see what she thinks about picking him up on some other woman's doorstep."

"I don't think his nose can take another hit tonight." He ran his thumb over her fingers. "Flex these for me."

She did, slowly and fully, but he didn't miss the slightly ragged edge to her exhale.

"Good. Got a bag of frozen peas?"

"Hello? I'm bleeding here…"

Beau gave him the same look he used to intimidate uncooperative idiots he encountered on the job. One-for-Three had the good sense to shut his trap.

"Go inside and take a seat at the table. No, don't tilt your head back—tilt it forward and pinch your nostrils right here." He demonstrated on himself, and then pointed at his door. Mitch followed instructions, muttering under his breath as he disappeared into the apartment.

He turned back to Savannah. She'd curled her fingers into a half-closed position again, which he imagined felt most comfortable about now. "You have something to use as an ice pack?"

"Yes, sir."

He ignored the sarcasm. "Use it. Keep your hand elevated,

ice on, and I'll be over soon to take care of you."

"You don't have to take care of me, Beau."

He aimed her toward her door, opened it for her, and used his body to more or less crowd her into her apartment. "It's my prerogative as your fiancé."

"Very funny."

"My ironic sense of humor is just one of the things you love about me."

"Right up there with your stubborn streak and bossy-pants attitude." She tried to look irritated, but he caught the way she battled to keep the corner of her mouth from tilting up.

Suddenly he was fighting the same battle. He turned toward his place and without looking back, told her, "Put some ice on that hand, Rocky." He suspected his back took an insult in the form of a rude face or hand gesture, but the thought only made him smile more.

Important takeaways: Savannah knew how to throw a punch, and One-for-Three had no chance of convincing her to give them a second try. He couldn't blame her. Not with those stats. But a tiny part of him recognized the outcome satisfied him more than it should have.

No complications, he reminded himself.

• • •

WTF? Mitch showed up at your apartment tonight?!

Savannah read the screen of her phone while she sat at her table with her right hand under a bag of frozen blueberries. She typed, *Yep*, in an attempt to keep up her end of the text exchange with Sinclair, who was stuck in traffic on her way into Atlanta.

She tried to add, "I had to be prevented from killing him," but only got as far as "I had to be prevent" — before she accidentally hit send. What popped up in the balloon read, *I had to be pregnant.*

Shit. She sucked at left-hand texting.

An emoji of a yellow face with hands pressed to its cheeks and mouth hanging open came back instantly.

Savannah leaned over her phone and typed more slowly. *Prevented! I had to be PREVENTED from killing him.*

Whew. Don't get me wrong, can't wait to be crazy Aunt Clair, but please not thanks to… The sentence ended with an emoji of what looked like a smiling pile of poop.

Never in a million years. Savannah was on the pill, and she always, without fail, used a condom as well. She wanted no surprises in that particular area of her life.

Did you tear his balls off and stomp on them?

I punched him in the face.

I love you.

She grinned, and added, *Maybe broke his nose.*

You're my hero.

A soft knock at her door interrupted her search for the flexing biceps emoji.

Gotta go. Drive safe. I'll see you soon.

She kicked her discarded boots out of her way, walked to the door, and opened it. Beau stood on the threshold, a big, rugged monument of testosterone in faded jeans and a gray crew neck with long sleeves pushed up lean, corded forearms. The slight throb in her knuckles took a backseat to a newer and far more distracting throb located nowhere in the vicinity of her hand. His gaze slid over her, slowly, and a muscle tensed in his jaw. She glanced down and studied herself through his eyes, taking in her bare feet, the thin strip of skin visible between the ruched-up hem of her layered tank tops and the low, hastily rolled waistband of her boyfriend jeans, the careless wisp of bubble-gum-pink lace peeking out from beneath the scooped neckline of her tanks.

Klassy. Do you wonder why Mitch never pictured you as Mrs. Mitchell Prescott III?

Cut it out, she silently ordered the negative voice in her head. Nobody blew glass in a Dior gown. It was a hot, sweaty, physical endeavor, and she loved it. A look at Beau told her he imagined a hot, sweaty, physical endeavor, too—the kind that put an anticipatory flush under his stubble-darkened cheeks and an untamed gleam in his eyes. The throb intensified, and every pulse point in her body got in on the action. When his attention shifted from the glimpse of pink lace to her lips, even her scalp prickled. Lost in the infinity of his wide, dark pupils, she lifted her hand to adjust her tank top, and winced.

The pain surprised her, and her quick inhale broke the spell. He frowned. "You're supposed to be icing that hand."

She let out a careful breath and backed up to let him in. "I was." A few steps brought her to the table. She lifted the bag of blueberries. "See."

He crossed the room slowly, closing in like a predator certain of its prey. His attention never wavered. When they stood almost toe-to-toe, he took her hand, cradled it in his larger, stronger one, and moved his thumb over her skin. "No cuts. That's good. Also next to no swelling around the fourth and fifth CMC joints." He lightly touched the landmarks at the base of her ring and little fingers.

"What's that mean?"

The corner of his mouth lifted. "It means you hit correctly. If you use this part of your fist"—he touched his thumb to the base of her ring and pinky fingers—"you get what we call a brawler's fracture."

"I'm unbreakable. My father would be proud."

"I'm not saying you don't have a break. You just don't have the most common closed-fist impact fracture. See this swelling right here?" He pointed to the sore red points at the base of her index and middle fingers. "You took a little damage."

"Yeah, well…you should see the other guy."

His lips curved again. "I have." Then he pressed on the area around one puffy knuckle a little harder than she expected, and looked at her—presumably to gauge her reaction. "Hurt?"

"Not too much."

"Sharp or dull?"

"Dull."

"How about this?" He did the same to the other knuckle.

"Same…so Mitch will live?" Not that he deserved a second thought from her, but her conscience insisted she ask.

"He's fine. You bruised his ego worse than his face." He tapped her hand. "Make a fist."

She complied. "Good to know, I guess."

He studied her balled fingers, lifting and turning her wrist to view her fist from various angles. "Okay. Open your hand completely and part your fingers as wide as you can." He demonstrated, and she followed his example. "You're not feeling sorry for him, are you? Or having second thoughts?"

"No. He blew his shot. To be honest, I don't know why I gave him one in the first place."

Beau took her fingers, one at a time, and gently pushed each toward the knuckle. "Because on paper he checked all the boxes…clean-cut, educated, gainfully employed, and not overly demanding of your time or attention."

"Ouch. When you sum it up like that, I sound really pathetic."

"Or really logical. You put a lot of yourself into your art, so you steer clear of guys who won't be happy unless your world revolves around them. Some people instinctively know where they need to draw the line—what they can offer, and what they can't. Not everyone is willing or able to invest everything they've got in a relationship."

Tidy notion, and maybe true to an extent with regard to Mitch, but it ignored one important fact. She needed her world to revolve around more than just her art, and refused to believe she wasn't capable of giving more. She wanted a true soul mate, and children someday, *and* her career. Was that so selfish? Deep down, didn't he need more, too? She wanted to ask, but her expression must have telegraphed her intention to turn the conversation to him, and apparently it wasn't a direction he wanted to take. He kept talking.

"Why you got involved isn't really my point. What I'm trying to pin down is how definite you feel about the breakup. Somewhere around the time your fist connected with his face, he got the hint you weren't interested in talking, but if you call and apologize, you're going to undermine the message. He'll think he has a chance. You wouldn't want to do that, would you?"

Long, competent fingers encircled her wrist, and his warm, hard palm slid against hers.

She shivered.

"No. I wouldn't." The words came out steady, even though her insides trembled. She couldn't take her eyes off the sight of his fingers around her wrist. Her other wrist tingled as if caught in his grasp, too. She imagined him lifting her arms over her head, pinning them there while he slowly lowered his mouth to hers.

He drew his hand back, running his fingertips over her palm as he retreated.

"What would you want to do, Savannah?"

Chapter Ten

Savannah's lips parted. She ran the tip of her tongue along the dip in her upper lip, and Beau strained his ears in the hopes of hearing her say, "I want you to fuck me, hard," over the pounding of his pulse.

The pounding came again, only louder, and her lips formed the words…

"I better get that."

Huh?

She walked past him and opened the front door. *Without* looking through the peephole. Sinclair stood on the other side of the threshold with a wheeled carry-on bag parked beside her. She leaned in and wrapped Savannah in a big hug. A bottle of wine dangled from one hand.

What the hell?

"Hey, sis. Since I didn't get your good news until after I-85 stole the better part of my evening, I stopped by the Circle K on my way here and splurged on a bottle of their finest"— she paused as her gaze landed on Beau—"which we can split three ways." Deep blue eyes looked him up and down.

"*Oooor* I could leave the wine and go get a bite to eat. The Waffle House on the corner stays open all night, right?"

"Shut up and get in here." Savannah made a move to grab the handle of Sinclair's bag with her good hand, but he crossed the room and shooed her away.

"I've got it." He hefted the luggage and placed it inside the door. "You moving in, Sinclair?"

"For one night. I've got an early flight out of Hartsfield-Jackson tomorrow morning. Savannah offered up half her Serta so I didn't have to wake up at the crack of dawn and make the drive."

So much for his prurient fantasies involving Savannah and her Serta. A brick of disappointment settled in his gut—or thereabouts—even though it was for the best. The "no complications" pledge remained in full force and effect. Getting physically involved with a woman who planned to dump him come the first of the year invited unnecessary tension into an already-tricky situation. The comparatively straightforward situation in his jeans persisted, but he had plenty of experience resolving that on his own. He eyed the bottle of wine in Sinclair's hand. "What are we celebrating?"

"Some fiancé you are. You don't even know your future wife got an offer to participate in a special exhibit at the Mercer Gallery?"

No, he didn't, and that probably seemed kind of odd. He glanced at Savannah. "Congratulations."

"Thanks, but you can stop racking your brain for a way to explain why you weren't the first to get the news. Sinclair's messing with you. She knows we're not really engaged. I told her last week because I didn't want her wasting time designing rings for us."

"Oh." Could Sinclair keep a secret?

Sinclair patted his arm as she walked past him on her way to the kitchen. "Don't worry. My lips are sealed." She put the wine on the counter and dug around in a drawer for a corkscrew.

Savannah went to the table and took a seat. He picked up the bag of blueberries and settled it across her knuckles. She gave him an exasperated look but left them there.

Sinclair brought the bottle, the corkscrew, and three glasses to the table. He commandeered the corkscrew and did the honors while Sinclair fussed over Savannah's hand.

"Dang, girl. You really nailed him, didn't you? Are you okay?"

"I'm fine. The paramedic who rushed to my rescue assured me nothing's broken, which is good because I've got a load of work to do between now and New Year's Eve."

He poured a glass of wine and pushed it to Savannah. "What happens New Year's Eve?"

"The Mercer hosts a series of showcases, kicking off on New Year's Eve. They spotlight artists to watch in the coming year, invite their best clients, curators from major museums, and buyers for private collections. After my gallery folded, I approached Mercer and had a really good meeting with the director. She felt me out about participating in a showcase, but mentioned they'd already finalized their featured artists for New Year's. This week a mixed-media artist they originally selected withdrew for personal reasons. They called me. I'm in."

Sinclair accepted the glass of wine he slid toward her and high-fived Savannah. "I told you they'd call. Which of your works are you going to exhibit?"

"Well, there's the thing. I have three large pieces I managed to get back from my old gallery before the Feds closed them down, but Mercer wants more—the manager told me the commission agreement they're sending will specify five additional works. Smaller scale, thank God, because I can create those mostly on my own, but I've got four weeks to work my magic. I'm going to be busy."

"Here's to busy." Sinclair raised her glass and tapped it to Savannah's. Beau poured a splash of wine into the third glass and did the same. Then he took a sip and immediately wished for a beer. Which he had, waiting for him across the hall in the bag of groceries he'd yet to put away. Time to head out.

He pushed the cork into the bottle and placed it in the middle of the table. "My work here is done. Sinclair, have a good flight." And then, to Savannah, he said, "Keep the ice on for another ten minutes, then take a break, then ice it for another ten before you go to bed."

"I will. Thanks for everything. Sorry for dragging you into my drama."

He shrugged off the apology and crossed to the door. Compared to the dramas he confronted on the job, hers barely fit the definition, but he was happy enough not to transport anybody to the ER—particularly her. "Being engaged to a paramedic comes with certain fringe benefits."

The comment earned him a smile, but then her eyes widened and she jumped up. "Speaking of which, being engaged to a glass artist comes with certain benefits, too. Hold on a minute."

He waited by the door while she ran to her bedroom, and returned in the promised minute carrying a package about the size of a shoe box. She handed it to him. "What's this?"

"Happy birthday."

Oh, right. The birthday present. The package suddenly felt much heavier in his hands. The idea of putting some colorful, breakable memento in his apartment tensed him up. He turned the box in his hands, looking for the easiest way to unwrap it. "Thanks."

Her laugh told him he failed at hiding his reservations about the gift. "I packed it pretty well. Open it at your place. But don't worry. It's small and unobtrusive, just like we discussed." She fiddled with his hair as she spoke, brushing it back from his forehead, and then his temples. Maybe he'd hold off on a trim.

"Okay." He opened the door and paused at the threshold. "See you later."

"No kiss goodnight?" Sinclair stared at the two of them expectantly.

He blew Sinclair a kiss, and walked back to his apartment. The birthday present went on his kitchen counter while he put the groceries away and popped the cap off a beer. He made a sandwich and ate it, rinsed the plate, loaded the dishwasher, and took care of a bunch of other small chores, all the while feeling oddly solitary. The mood irritated him, because he *liked* his space, dammit. He got all the interaction he needed at work, and plenty of chaos to go with it. At home, he preferred calm. Quiet. Order. He enjoyed control of his environment.

The box on the counter caught his eye. He finished his beer, tossed the empty, and rubbed his palms on his jeans. Then he reached for the box. And hesitated. Every colorful, cluttered inch of Savannah's apartment flashed through his mind. Not a calm, orderly space.

Shit. This thing was going to stick out like a neon rainbow in his apartment.

It's temporary. You can put it in a closet after your parents visit.

Right. He used a letter opener to cut through the tape across the top of the box, dug into a bunch of Styrofoam peanuts, and pulled out...a blue blown-glass vase. A bouquet of spiral-petaled daisies bloomed out the top, and a sneaky, iridescent green snake curled around the vase, from the base to the neck.

He felt his lips twitch as he slowly turned it, viewing the thing from all sides. Very funny. And fitting. And a guy like him could appreciate the practicality, because these flowers would never die.

. . .

Sinclair stood in the doorway between the bedroom and the bathroom, her toothbrush loaded up with toothpaste, and pointed it at Savannah. "So, what's the status with you and Beau?"

Savannah paused in the act of rummaging through her tall dresser for something to sleep in. "You know the status. We're neighbors, childhood friends, and I'm helping convince his parents they don't need to worry about him."

Sinclair rolled her eyes and retreated into the bathroom to rinse. From the sink, she called, "You've omitted key details from your report."

Savannah found an old Bulldogs T-shirt she'd scored from a boyfriend in college, yanked off her tank tops, shrugged out of her bra, and pulled on the weathered red cotton. "Such as?"

Her sister poked her head out the bathroom door. "Such as I practically burst into flames every time he looks at you — and he looks at you constantly. It's a miracle I'm not bruised from wandering into the middle of all the eye-banging."

Thank God Sinclair disappeared into the bathroom again, because Savannah felt heat seep into her cheeks. She wiggled out of her jeans and stepped into a pair of gray cut-off sweatpants. "You have an overactive imagination."

"Oh, please." Sinclair swept into the room, wearing black flannel sleep pants with grinning white skulls on them and a black camisole. "The sexual tension between you two might as well have been a fourth person in the room. A really horny fourth person."

"We're pretending to be engaged..."

"Not to me, you're not, so don't try to tell me it's an act.

Anyway, for the sake of the charade, you need to find a way to release some of the tension."

"What? Why?" She got into bed. "An engaged couple ought to throw off a little heat, don't you think?"

Sinclair dug her hairbrush out of her overnight bag. "Heat yes, but not nonstop sparks of hungry anticipation—"

"Maybe we're holding out until our wedding night?"

"Um...no. Sorry." She ran the brush through her hair. "Nobody's going to believe that."

"Well, jeez, thanks a lot."

"Come on, Savannah. You're both pushing thirty…"

"I'm twenty-seven!"

"Exactly. And you've been in several serious relationships. Beau's been married. It's too late for either of you to take a virginity pledge."

"So what are you suggesting? I march over there, knock on his door, and say, *Hey, we need to have sex because right now it's painfully obvious we haven't, and our families are going to know something's not right*?"

"You're attracted to him, aren't you?"

"Sinclair, believe it or not, I don't have sex with every guy I'm attracted to."

"But this is a unique situation."

"It's also a temporary one. This 'engagement'"—she made air quotes—"ends in January, and we agreed not to complicate things. Why risk the messy emotional fallout?"

"You talk like having sex automatically leads to complications. I beg to differ. Sometimes it's just about attraction, affection, and fun. Neither party expects more, and everybody walks away happy." She shrugged. "Two people enjoying one of life's little perks. Safely and responsibly, of course."

Sinclair spoke from experience. As far as Savannah could tell, her sister focused exclusively on attraction, affection, and fun. She had her own theories about why her little sister avoided anything more, but now wasn't the time to delve into them unless she wanted to drag them both through some extremely messy emotions.

But maybe, in this case, Sinclair had a point. "Enjoy a little perk, huh?"

A knock from the other side of the wall made her jump.

Sinclair stepped back from the bed. "What the hell was that?"

"Beau," she mouthed, and then pointed at the wall behind her and whispered, "His bedroom is on the other side."

Her sister looked at the wall. "Do you think he heard us?"

She lifted a shoulder. *Who knows?*

Sinclair climbed onto the bed, leaned her face close to the wall, and motioned for Savannah to do the same.

"Good night on three," she whispered, and used her fingers to tick off the count.

In unison they called out, "Good night, Beau!"

"Good night, Smiths," he called back.

Sinclair grinned and crawled under the blankets. Savannah did the same, and then clicked off her bedside light, plunging the room into darkness.

A voice through the wall disrupted the silence. "For the record, there's nothing little about my perk."

Chapter Eleven

Beau glanced at Savannah's door as he climbed the steps to his apartment. UPS had left a letter-sized cardboard envelope on her welcome mat. He'd bet his last beer it contained the fellowship packet she was waiting for, including her travel stipend and airline tickets. He turned to his apartment, but then hesitated. Her doorstep seemed like a bad place to leave important documents.

A glance at his watch told him it wasn't quite eight o'clock. She might work for another four or five hours. He could take the envelope to his place for safekeeping, but he knew she was anxious to receive the information. He could call and let her know it had arrived, but they'd called and texted enough in the past few days for him to know that if she was working she wouldn't pick up.

Just drive over to the studio and deliver the damn thing. It wasn't as if he had plans for tonight, and he'd been meaning to take her up on her invitation to watch her work. When they had dinner with his parents tomorrow, he ought to be able to speak coherently about her process.

And he was spending a lot of mental energy justifying a simple decision. Yes, he liked the idea of seeing her this evening. So what? He turned and headed downstairs to his car before he could waste any more time debating this move like a thirteen-year-old girl.

The studio wasn't far. He had a general idea of the location, but as the restaurants, grocery stores, and mini malls transitioned to more of an industrial district, the idea of Savannah working at night got a lot less appealing. The small parking lot in front of the studio was decently lit, at least. He parked his Yukon next to her Explorer, grabbed the envelope, and took the steps to the heavy doors of the two-story brick warehouse. Music ambushed him as soon as he stepped through. From invisible speakers, a deep-voiced singer begged someone to take him to church, loud enough to rattle the cement block walls.

Inside, a series of dormant utilitarian workstations divided the open space into sections. The north and south walls each held a pair of furnaces—one large, one smaller—and before one of the small furnaces stood Savannah.

He walked closer, the music obscuring the sound of his footsteps on the concrete floor. A pair of sunglasses shielded her eyes as she stared into the furnace. She had her hair pulled up in a bundle at the back of her head, and wore faded jeans that clung to her ass like a second skin, along with a snug white T-shirt bearing a Marble City Glassworks logo across the back with the words "Best Blow Job in Tennessee" emblazoned in big black letters below the logo.

The glow from the furnace turned her skin gold. She held one end of a long, narrow pipe in the round opening at the front of the furnace, twirling it at a constant rate. After a moment she stepped back, removing the length of pipe from the furnace, and bringing a molten glob of red-hot glass out of the heat. Still twirling the rod steadily, she brought the other end to her lips. Her chest rose as she inhaled. Then she blew into the pipe. The glob expanded like a lopsided balloon, but quickly evened into a sphere as she continued to twist and blow.

He watched her hands as she worked, and her lips, mesmerized by the assurance with which she finessed the delicate balance between air and gravity. Mesmerized...and turned on. Her fingers danced along the metal shaft, and he imagined those deft fingertips touching his skin. She closed her lips around the end of the pipe, pursing them slightly to ensure a tight seal, and his cock begged for the same treatment.

No complications.

What's so complicated about two consenting adults tearing the clothes off each other and fucking until they can't stand?

Uh-uh. No way. This was not an argument he was going to have with himself. She inspired a dangerous mix of gratitude, affection, and lust, but they'd both be better off not blurring the boundaries of their arrangement with a physical relationship. That was not the plan.

A bead of sweat trickled between his shoulder blades when she slid the rod from between her lips and absently licked them as she considered the glass. Apparently satisfied, she shoved her sunglasses up to the top of her head and turned toward a large table with a stainless steel top. Then she spotted him and lost her grip on the pipe. It clattered to the floor, and the molten mass at the end splattered on the concrete like a burst bubble.

He closed the space between them, to make sure she was okay, and apologize for scaring her, and yeah, to read her the riot act for working alone in an unlocked studio at this time of night. But somewhere around the moment he got close enough to touch her, his self-control shattered as irrevocably as the glass. All those plans fell away under the force of a different imperative.

Don't...

He tossed the envelope on the table, sank his hands into her upswept hair, and kissed her.

Soft lips parted beneath his, and her half thankful, half desperate groan flowed into his mouth. Her hands grappled for holds on his shoulders, and her leg twined around his, the heel of her boot digging into his calf as she tried to climb him. The height difference worked against them, but he had a solution. He hauled her up and carried her over to the table.

She landed on the solid surface harder than he intended, because he had no finesse left in him. He'd tamped down on this need for too long, and now it owned him. But she didn't seem to mind—simply pulled his head down and sank her teeth into his lower lip while her hands found his fly and tore it open. When she reached in to touch him, he intercepted. Later, when he wasn't about to explode, she could touch all she wanted, but for now he moved her arms behind her, then grasped her hips and lifted them so she had no choice but to brace her hands on the table to support her weight.

The music ended, leaving them in an echoing silence. He dragged her jeans and underwear down to her knees, but that wasn't going to be enough. "Your boots," he muttered.

"Lace-ups. I can't wait. Find another way."

All right. He was nothing if not a problem solver. He pulled her off the table and spun her around. Her sunglasses flew off, skittered across the table, and landed on the floor.

"I owe you a new pair," he ground out.

"I don't care." She gripped the steel sides, leaned over, and parted her legs as far as the jeans would allow.

The sight of her lifting that perfect little ass to receive him made any lingering hopes of mustering up some foreplay impossible. He curled one hand around the base of his cock, the other around her hip, and drove in.

The first thrust jostled a loud "Yes!" out of her, rocked

her onto her tiptoes, and sent her hands scrambling across the top of the table for a more secure hold. She steadied herself and arched her back in time to meet his second thrust. Flesh slapped against flesh.

She cried out again, but he wasn't so far gone or so out of practice he failed to realize he'd given her nothing yet except a rough pounding. He needed to do better than what had become his MO—a quick, mind-numbing release, followed by an immediate exit.

Make it good for her, so she'll let you have her again.

Again?

Hell yes, again. Your mind's not numb this time, and you know damn well there's no immediate exit.

Instead of suffocating him, the realization grounded him. Focused him. There was an eventual exit, they both knew it, and the shared awareness made this recklessness okay. Repeatable, even, provided he did something worth repeating. A thousand ideas raged through his mind—touch her breasts and figure out if she liked a gentle stroke or a firm caress. Slide his hand between her legs and determine if she preferred the graze of his finger on her clit or a hard grind against his palm.

Unfortunately, they would have to wait, because the hot, tight hug of her body felt too good to do anything except thrust again.

Tension gathered in his gut, his balls. The backs of his thighs burned. Neurons fired at will, taking direction from some primitive part of his brain his conscious mind couldn't touch, leaving him a passenger in his own body. His thrusts turned fast and reckless, and there wasn't a damn thing he could do to slow the train down. Fuck. He was done for.

"Next time, Savannah. Next time, I swear to God, I'm going to rain orgasms on you until you drown in your own pleasure, but right now I have to—"

She threw back her head and screamed while inner muscles dissolved into a frenzy of contractions around him. They squeezed the orgasm right out of him in a rush so sudden and violent he would have collapsed if the table hadn't been there to support him.

Holy shit.

It took a minute for him to catch his breath and reestablish motor control. Then he braced his weight on his forearms, turned his head, and kissed the corner of her smiling mouth. The off-center smile got him every time.

"Sorry I interrupted your work."

Her husky laugh tickled his skin. "Oh yeah. Me, too." With that, she tucked her hands under her shoulders and started to push herself upright, but he didn't budge.

"Don't move, Smith. I'm not done with you yet."

• • •

Not done with her yet? He'd just made her come so hard she might have broken something. She raised her head to ask what else he could possibly do to her, but he chose that moment to slowly drag his extremely effective cock from her pleasure-swollen body. She bit her lip and groaned as he withdrew, unable to stop herself from wringing a last few greedy spasms of satisfaction from the process.

When he finally slipped free, she sighed and started to straighten, but a big hand splayed across the center of her back and held her still. "Uh-uh. I told you not to move."

He wanted her to just…lean over a table, half naked? She wasn't especially shy, but the idea of lying there bare and trembling from aftershocks made her blush. She felt displayed. Exposed.

And yet the uncomfortable experience of holding herself still for his perusal made her so hot she could hardly keep still.

Where was he looking? What could he see?

Just when the tension of the moment became unbearable, warm, firm lips trailed over the vulnerable curve of her ass cheek. She nearly jumped out of her skin, but a hand at the small of her back kept her still while he scraped his teeth along sensitive territory.

"I've been fantasizing about kissing this ass since I saw it naked, in my bed, Friday morning."

At the same time he delivered the revelation, his fingers delved between her thighs and searched out the still-quivering spot that reduced her to a slave with one featherlight touch.

Those nimble fingertips stroked again, and she pursued the fleeting caress in a blind effort to prolong the addictive agony. He rewarded her effort by sinking his teeth into her flesh, and her bones dissolved. She gripped the sides of the table to keep from sliding to the floor.

Sweet Jesus, Savannah. The man just bit your ass. She loved a helping hand every once in a while. What woman didn't? But who knew she'd be so susceptible to a good, sound biting? Now she had two competing punishments to withstand: the unbearable assault of his fingers teasing her clit, and the irresistible sting of his teeth against her unguarded flesh. Should she beg for mercy, or plead for more?

He gave her more, biting and stroking while she chased an increasingly crucial release, and yet for some reason she never saw the orgasm coming until those gentle fingers and not-so-gentle teeth shot her up and over a ragged crest.

Before her breathing evened out, his voice filled her ear. "Again."

He didn't give her a chance to respond—not with words. Instead, jostled a gasp out of her when he flipped her over and laid her on the table again. She propped herself up on her elbows, and realized she'd just had two screaming orgasms with her shirt and shoes on. Hell, technically, she still qualified for service in finer fast-food restaurants throughout Atlanta. But Beau intended to change that. She watched as he knelt by her dangling feet and got to work on her laces.

The *clomp* of one boot hitting the floor reached her ears. Another *clomp* told her he'd tossed the second boot.

Then he peeled her jeans off and gave her a look that sent waves of hot and cold over every inch of her exposed skin. "Beau…I appreciate the effort, sincerely, but I'm not sure I've got more in me at the moment."

"You're wrong. Give me a minute and I'll show you." He propped her heels on his shoulders.

She gripped the edge of the table and decided the least she could do was let him prove his point. "Okay. I'll give you a minute. I'm a giver."

As a reward, he licked and bit his way to her navel, over her abdomen, shoving her T-shirt out of his way as he went. When he'd pushed the garment up to her armpits, he caught a handful of the front, pulled her upright, and jerked the shirt over her head. Her bra came, too, and ended up tangled with her shirt around her wrists. She tried to slip her hands free and realized she couldn't. He'd fashioned an effective if unintentional restraint.

Or maybe not unintentional at all, she corrected when their eyes met. His hands cupped her breasts, lifting their weight, bringing one aching peak dangerously close to his mouth. "Can you come for me this way?"

And in that moment, she didn't just want to come again. She wanted to come *for him*, while he alternated between kissing the tender undersides of her breasts and sucking her nipples until she felt the pull of his mouth in every last cell of her body.

"I don't know. Usually I need more"—she broke off as he took her nipple into his mouth and drew on it hard enough to bow her spine—"God, maybe."

Keeping the suction tight, he slowly drew back, millimeter by millimeter, until her breast popped free. Sensations spiraled through her, sharp and almost painful. She nearly cried out, but then his mouth returned, gentle this time. He kissed the soft, sensitive curve where her breast met her torso, slowly worked his way up the swell to where her nipple jutted, tight and throbbing. His lips barely touched the tip, and every muscle below her belly button clenched.

Halfway through withstanding the same sweet torture to her other breast, impatience and need reached a critical point. She couldn't keep her hands still, pulling and twisting to free them from the trap of her shirt. She couldn't keep her legs still, either. Open thighs. Closed thighs. Nothing eased the pressure between them. Finally, she broke.

"I can't," she panted, and squeezed her eyes shut and parted her restless legs. "I need to feel you inside me."

His palms slid up her thighs, parting them wider and holding them open. "What would you like? My fingers? My tongue?"

She couldn't think. "Either. Both. Anything."

"My cock?"

Was that an option? So soon? "Yes." She fluttered her legs against his hands. "If you can. You don't have to be super hard... Oh!"

He was inside her before she finished speaking, and hardness? Not an issue. Then he brought his face close to hers, and growled, "Yes. I do. Unlike what's-his-name, I don't use sex to jack off my ego. I wouldn't waste your time, or the privilege of your body, with some weak, self-serving fuck. I give you my best whenever I'm inside you. Nothing but my best." He emphasized each word with a deep thrust, and her eyes watered with gratitude. "Or I find another way to make you come. Are we clear?"

She struggled to find her voice, to say "Yes, sir!" or "Thank you," or quite possibly, "Praise Jesus, hallelujah." God only knew what would actually fly out of her mouth, but before she could speak, his moves got faster, and all she could do was loop her arms around his neck, wrap her legs around his hips, and hold on.

She might have had a shot at being more than a clinging ride-along if he'd stuck with a steady rhythm, but he kept her guessing, alternating between lightning-quick thrusts and slow, deep, breath-stealing plunges. Playing with her. Every time she thought she found the right pace, he changed it.

He put his mouth to work on her breasts, obviously not ready to abandon plan A completely, and she nearly levitated off the table. Maybe some part of her did, because although her eyes refused to open, she suddenly saw herself lying there, a sweaty, shaking mess with her hair spilled all over, and the rest of her clamped around Beau as if he anchored her world. Was this what people meant by an out-of-body experience?

Beyond the sound of her heartbeat thundering in her ears, she heard her own voice. Not polite, seductively encouraging requests like, *Oh baby, you're so good. Do that again,* but raw, inarticulate pleas littered with moans and curses. Her pleas. Her moans. Her curses.

She really ought to get herself under control, but it was too late. Her body had shirked off whatever leash her mind had on it, and only obeyed its new master.

And sweet Jesus, the man knew his tricks. Big hands closed around her wrists and pulled her arms back until they rested on the table above her head. He levered himself up, unwrapped her legs from his waist, and for one moment of pure panic, she thought he'd finished and intended to leave. Relief washed through her when he hitched her legs over his shoulders. The new position put him deeper than ever, and wiped all lingering self-consciousness from her mind.

She'd cry, beg, sweat, and shake — whatever it took to ride

this to completion and live. Calves draped over his shoulders, weight shifted to the center of her back, she offered him unrestricted access to everything.

He fully exploited the access, slamming hard against her quivering flesh with every thrust, then rolling his hips to give her a perfect grind while leaving her enough wiggle room to drive herself a little bit insane with every withdrawal.

"Look at me, Savannah."

The husky directive tripped some self-preservation alarm she didn't even realize she'd installed. Giving him free rein over her body was one thing, but staring into Beau Montgomery's eyes while she surrendered every last bit of control to him suddenly struck her as dangerously intimate.

She kept her eyes closed and assumed her silent refusal would be the end of it. She assumed wrong.

A hand cupped her jaw and tipped her face up. His chest scraped her overstimulated nipples for a torturous moment before his pecs settled on her breasts. Determined lips covered hers, parted them wide while his tongue whipped hers into submission, and then stroked a hot, wandering path through every unprotected recess, persuasive and demanding at the same time. When he suddenly abandoned the kiss, shock forced her eyes open, and she promptly fell into his.

He shot her a tight-lipped grin. "I'm about to give you your third orgasm of the night. That calls for a little eye contact. In fact, I'm pretty sure you're going to say my name before it's over."

Was that all he wanted? No problem. "My name."

Chapter Twelve

Beau couldn't remember the last time he'd laughed while an orgasm bore down on him like the wrath of God. Then Savannah rocked her hips, grazing his balls with the underside of her ass, and annihilated all the restraint he had left. His laughter died in his throat. He thrust again, and again, racing toward relief with an urgency that left zero room for artful fucking. No more teasing shifts in tempo, no clit-thrilling flourishes, just a driving need to pound them both into oblivion as quickly as possible.

She bucked under him, tensed her legs, and arched up as the orgasm gripped her. Her whole body clamped around him, vibrating with the strain.

Every fiber in him screamed to move, to surge, to do whatever it took to feel her tight embrace along the length of his shaft.

Wait. Wait for it…

She arched higher, taking him infinitesimally deeper, and froze. Her voice cracked as she cried his name, and ended in a long, thankful moan. He reveled in the triumph for half a

"We hang out at your place. Your parents have already seen my bedroom, so they're going to know we use yours."

"Then they know more than I know."

Men. She took him by the hand, led him to the bedroom, and gestured. "What do you see?"

"My bedroom."

"Dominated by what?"

Now he frowned. "My bed?"

"Exactly. Your big, roomy California king. I have a standard queen. You're what, six three? Tell me, Beau, which bed do we use?"

"Mine."

"Damn right we do." She reached into her bag, pulled out a red silk nightie, and chucked it at the head of the bed. It spilled across the white pillowcases. Satisfied with the effect, she headed into the adjoining bathroom and began unloading the last remaining items in her bag. She placed a toothbrush in the glass holder next to Beau's, lined up her face cleanser, moisturizer, and perfume on the counter, and then placed shampoo, conditioner, body wash, and a razor in the metal caddy hanging from the showerhead. When she opened the medicine cabinet, she caught a glimpse of Beau's face in the reflection.

Her disk of birth control pills fit perfectly on the narrow shelf, between a bottle of Visine and a box of Band-Aids.

"Savannah, they're not going to search the place in the time it takes to have a drink and then head out for an early dinner. Ditto for pie and coffee afterwards. They'll be here an hour, tops."

She shut the cabinet and faced him in the mirror. "Moms are nosy. Trust me, Cheryl checks your medicine cabinet every time she visits."

He reached past her, opened the cabinet, and grabbed a bottle of ibuprofen. In the time it took her to turn around he dry-swallowed two. "Headache?"

"Call me crazy, but something about the idea of my mom snooping through my medicine cabinet hurts my brain."

"You look a little pale." Concerned, she reached up and touched his forehead. "Do you think you're coming down with something?"

"No. It's…" He trailed off and his eyes drifted to the counter, then the shower, then back to her. "It's been a while since I shared space with things like this." He touched her perfume. "Brings back memories."

Shit. She'd been so intent on setting the scene to make the proper impact on his parents, she hadn't stopped to consider the impact on him. "You know what? This is overkill." She reached for the bottles on the counter, but he caught her hand.

"Leave them." He glanced around again and nodded. "You're right—every detail. It just took me by surprise. I never envisioned what this place would look like if I were involved with someone."

"Because you never envisioned getting involved again?" Now wasn't the time, and his bathroom wasn't the place for this conversation, but she couldn't hold back the question.

He leaned back against the counter, crossed his arms, and let out a long, tired breath. "Not really, no."

"That's crazy. You're not even thirty. Would your wife have expected you to live like a monk for the rest of your life?"

"You can take the halo off my head, Savannah. I haven't lived like a monk. But no, Kelli would have expected me to mourn for a decent amount of time, and then move on and let some new woman enjoy all the hard work she sank into training me to put the toilet seat down."

A glance at the toilet confirmed Kelli had trained him well. "So why haven't you?" She asked the question quietly.

"Because I can't go all-in again."

"I don't understand." But she wanted to. She touched his forearm and felt a muscle jump.

"Losing Kelli left a scar—a bad one—but losing our daughter…" He looked down, and took a deep breath before continuing. "I don't really have the words to describe the loss, but it's true what they say. A parent should never have to bury a child. Losing Abbey hurtled me down a very deep, very dark rabbit hole, and hitting bottom broke something inside me. I can't fix it."

"That's a father grieving, but, Beau, you're still a father. All those paternal instincts? All the love? They're there, waiting for—"

"No." He jerked his head up, and she almost backed away from the desolation in his eyes. "I can't. I don't have the capacity to withstand that kind of loss a second time. Maybe other people do, but I don't."

"Maybe you wouldn't have to," she pointed out as gently as possible. "Maybe the next time around is its own unique, completely different experience?"

"Unfortunately, I can't get past the 'maybe' risk." He dragged a hand through his hair. "I see the wrong side of 'maybe' all the time on the job. Nobody's immune. And just in case I started to forget that little fact, my mom got hit with a cancer diagnosis."

She smoothed his hair off his forehead and wished she could smooth away his worry as easily. "Beau, your mom's going to be okay."

He captured her hand and gave it a squeeze. "I hope so. Her doctors say things like good probability of a surgical cure, and low likelihood of recurrence, but words like 'probability' and 'likelihood' basically amount to different versions of 'maybe.'"

She took the hand holding hers and turned it palm up. "Did you know in addition to my Master of Fine Arts, I'm also a master of the ancient science of palm reading?"

"You're a woman of many talents. I didn't realize the University of Georgia offered the degree."

"This one's courtesy of the University of YouTube, but a lot of people would argue it's more valuable than the MFA." She ran her index finger over his palm, letting her nail trace the long, measured curve bracketing his thumb. "This is your lifeline."

"Do that again and some things are definitely going to spring to life."

"Keep it in your pants, Montgomery. I'm working here. See these tiny lines intersecting the lifeline?"

He leaned in, bringing his face close to hers, and her mind took an unauthorized trip back to last night, to the heat of his mouth on her skin and the slide of his tongue.

"Yes," he answered, but she got the feeling his reply addressed the all-too-clear invitation her hormones issued rather than her question.

"Focus, please. These little lines signify points where a guardian angel entered your life. You've got one way down here, when you were small—four or five. Maybe a grandparent or family friend passed?"

Narrowed eyes found hers. "My grandfather died when I was five."

"There you go."

"Someone mentioned it to you recently, or you remember from back then—"

"Or I'm a master palmist. Either way, the lines don't lie. It's there. You've got two more here," she pointed to the pair intersecting his lifeline farther along. "We know who they are."

"Okay, and your point?"

"You don't pick up any more guardian angels until way down here." She ran her finger along the line, toward his wrist, circled the next line, and then folded his hand, held it in both of hers, and planted a kiss on his knuckles. "Your mom's going to be fine. So are you."

"The lines don't lie, huh?"

"Never. Now that we've eliminated the pesky maybes from your future, what will you do? The coast is clear the next time you're tempted to go all-in."

"Maybe the coast is clear because I keep it clear?"

"For a man who hates 'maybe', you sure find your way back to the word quickly."

"Because I don't need any more guardian angels." He gave her a grim smile. "And I do need to stay out of the rabbit hole."

"Helloooo? Anybody home?"

"Showtime," Beau said, and then called out, "Come in. We'll be right there."

She folded her shopping bag and shoved it into the cabinet under the sink, banking her frustration over the premature end to their conversation while she was at it. Though really, was the end premature? He'd been honest, and who was she to tell him how he should feel or what he should do? She hadn't walked in his shoes.

Even so, the persistent voice in the back of her mind kept insisting he sold himself short.

So be it, she decided as she followed him to the living area. He hadn't asked her to change him, or fix him. She was helping him out, and enjoying some extremely cathartic rebound sex in the process. But as she watched him kiss his mom and hug his father, the annoying voice spoke up again.

Nice try, but this goes beyond a favor or rebound sex. You're invested. You care.

Chapter Thirteen

Beau scraped the feet of his chair against black and white octagonal tiles of the restaurant floor as he pushed back from the table. He crossed his arms and tried to emulate his father's calm expression while his mom chatted matter-of-factly about going under a surgeon's knife in a week to remove cancer from her body.

If he pulled off the outward calm, he deserved an Academy Award. While he waded into grisly scenes on a routine basis at work without so much as a hard swallow, the idea of his mom's surgery made his head pound, his palms sweat, and the full rack of Memphis-rubbed ribs he'd just finished threaten a stampede. The restaurant filled with young families and retirees at this early hour suddenly seemed too loud and way too hot. The trademark red-and-white-striped decor boasted holiday flourishes in addition to the normal overload of vintage signs and regional memorabilia, and the exuberance of color attacked his retinas.

A slim, cool hand slid over one of his. Savannah. She was a sight for sore eyes, with her blonde curls cascading down the back of her slouchy black sweater, one shoulder on display courtesy of the wide neckline. Skinny white jeans clung to her slim thighs and disappeared into the tops of high black suede boots.

The boots had launched an armada of fantasies when he'd seen her standing at his door tonight, but now he felt nothing but gratitude as she sat next to his mom, listening attentively while she casually swept her fingertips along his tense knuckles. He uncrossed his arms and took her hand, wove his fingers between hers, and held tight. She spared him a warm glance and a quick smile before turning again to his mom and saying, "I can't believe it's an outpatient procedure."

His mom nodded. "The tumor is small and there's no sign the cancer has spread, so I'm looking at simple lumpectomy and a sentinel lymph node dissection. The procedure itself will take less than an hour. Then I go to recovery, wake up, get dressed, and this handsome fellow"—she gestured to his dad—"takes me home. The next week I'll have a follow-up appointment with my surgeon, but assuming clear margins and no cancer present in the lymph nodes, I'm done."

Assuming. Another word he disliked. Assuming clear margins and negative lymph nodes didn't guarantee such an outcome. Falling short of assumptions meant additional, much more invasive surgery, maybe chemotherapy, radiation, and years of maintenance medications. Again, with no guarantees. The vital, energetic woman who'd bandaged his skinned knees and nursed his every fever when he was a kid might be embarking on a long, painful battle with a killer, and there was nothing he could do about it. He *hated* feeling so helpless.

"The surgery happens next Tuesday?" Savannah asked, and gave his hand a squeeze. The gesture made him realize he'd been holding hers tightly. Probably too tightly. He forced his fingers to relax and attempted to draw away. She stilled his retreat without missing a beat in her conversation with his mom. "I'll come with Beau to the hospital."

"You have the meeting with the gallery on Tuesday," he reminded her.

"I'll move it." She ran her short, unpainted fingernails along his wrist.

"No, please don't, sweetie," his mom interjected. "You either, Beau. I'm going to be a groggy, loopy mess after surgery. I'd just as soon have no witnesses."

"Except me," his father said, and kissed his mom's cheek.

"You made the 'for better or for worse' pledge, so you're exempt."

"I happen to like you loopy," he replied.

"Then you'll like me a lot on Tuesday."

"You'll call and let me know how it goes?" Beau asked, well aware his parents' decision had less to do with his mom's vanity and more to do with their desire to spare him memories of sitting in another hospital, waiting to learn the fate of his loved ones. He appreciated the intent, but couldn't help feeling somewhat shut out.

Had he made them feel shut out during the past three years? Probably, and he owed them an apology for keeping them at a distance, but now wasn't the time to dredge up their sad past. Instead he concentrated on Savannah's touch, even more so when those nimble fingers absently brushed over his cords, and then wandered back for another stroke. The conversation flowed around him while she smoothed the ridged cotton he'd deliberately chosen on a hunch she couldn't resist the soft fabric. The hunch paid off, and now the restaurant felt too hot for entirely different reasons. Out of self-defense he moved their hands to her lap, and enjoyed the feel of her slim thigh through her jeans. She stuttered on whatever she was saying to his mom, and her cheeks turned pink.

Oblivious to the game going on under the table, his mom

kept talking. "Trent's going to be in California the week following my surgery—"

"Cheryl, I told you I'd send Wagner to see the client."

"Don't be silly. Wagner's wife is going to pop out a baby any second. He can't go to California."

"I don't want you making the drive alone."

His mom had made the drive to Atlanta on her own plenty of times, but Beau understood his dad's sudden overprotectiveness. He pulled up his work schedule in his mind, and figured the feasibility of driving his mom to and from her appointment.

"Laurel volunteered to come with me. She had a really great idea, actually." His mom's eyes slid back to Savannah, and they twinkled with excitement. "She suggested we meet up with you after my appointment and spend the afternoon shopping for your wedding dress."

Savannah's cheeks went from pink to what he recognized as a guilty red, but to anyone else she looked like a blushing bride-to-be. "Oh. Well...I—"

"Mom, she's kind of slammed right now preparing for an important exhibit at the end of the month."

He meant to provide Savannah with a graceful out, but felt like an ass when his mom's face fell. Before he could offer to treat her and Mrs. Smith to lunch that day, Savannah patted his hand and spoke up. "I'd love to, actually. I've made good progress with my exhibit. I can afford an afternoon off."

"Wonderful!" His mom bounced in her chair like an excited teenager, and a wave of gratitude toward his "fiancée" rushed through him. Mom needed something fun to look forward to, and apparently spending an afternoon traipsing through the bridal salons of Atlanta qualified.

She leaned toward Savannah. "What style of dress are you partial to?"

He didn't hear her reply—and probably wouldn't have

understood it anyway—because his dad grinned at him and said, "Gee, Beau, what style of suit are you partial to?"

"Whatever style she tells me to get."

"Smart man. Bill and I refuse to shirk on our fatherly duties, though. Do we need to take you suit shopping at some point? And by 'suit shopping,' I mean eighteen holes at Stone Mountain."

He returned his dad's grin. "Sounds like a plan." Especially since he had no need for a suit.

"We'll put something together after the holidays." His dad's attention drifted to the flat-screen over the bar.

Across the restaurant a little blond boy no older than five sat at a table with his mom, another woman, and a little girl in a high chair. While the boy stared at the TV, he gripped the edge of the table, and rocked his chair onto its rear legs. Back, then forward. Back again. Beau stared, trying to catch the mom's attention, but the two women were deep in conversation. As the kid rocked forward, the back legs slipped on the tile floor. The chair skidded out from under him. The little guy flew forward and smacked his head against the table on the way to the ground.

The mom was on her knees cradling her son against her chest before the first wail went up. As soon as it did, waitresses hurried over. A few nearby diners offered napkins to the other woman at the table, who tried to mop up their spilled drinks before her friend got completely drenched. Then the mom drew back to check the damage, and cried out as well. Blood stained her light blue sweater and streamed down the boy's face.

Beau got up.

• • •

Savannah tailed Beau across the room toward the screaming

boy and distraught mom, almost barreling into him when he paused at a wait station to snag a handful of the restaurant's signature red napkins. He reached the table before her, his long strides eating up the distance without seeming to hurry. She skidded to a stop behind him as he knelt across from mom and son.

"Hi. My name's Beau, and I'm a paramedic. Mind if I take a look?"

"Please." The mom glanced up at him, her face a mask of panic. "Please help."

He moved closer to the boy, who clung to his mother, his little hand blocking the wound. "Hey, buddy, what's your name?"

"Liam," his mom replied. "His name is Liam. Oh my God. So much blood. Should I call an ambulance?"

"Let's have a look first."

Liam whimpered at that suggestion and aimed wide, wary eyes at Beau.

"William." His mom took hold of his little arm and tried to pull his hand away from his head. "Let the man see—"

Beau shook his head at the mom to stop her tug-of-war with her son. "Liam, how old are you?"

"He's five."

"Five an' a half," Liam corrected with a sniffle.

"So you're a pretty big boy." He slid his phone out of his pocket and hit a couple keys. "Do you play *Minecraft*?"

"Uh-huh, b-but I loosed my pri-pribleges 'cause I gave Kitty a haircut."

Beau's lips curved at the confession, and Savannah felt some of her worry drain away. He wouldn't smile and talk video games with the kid in the midst of a true medical crisis. Would he?

"Well, that'll definitely do it," Beau sympathized. "But this is a special circumstance. Think Mom will grant a temporary reprieve?"

"Of course," she said.

"Awesome." He held his phone out to the boy. "We're in creative mode and this looks like a really good world. I see trees, and water, and...hey...are those cows or pigs?"

Liam reached for the phone with both hands. "Pigs! See? They're pink."

Beau adjusted the screen higher, so Liam was forced to raise his head. "You gotta hold it up here. How many pigs do you see?" He asked the question while he gently moved Liam's blood-matted bangs away from his forehead.

"Tons." He tapped the screen repeatedly. "I'm building a fence 'round them."

"Good thinking. While you do that, I'm going to check your head, okay?"

"'Kay," he said, still tapping the screen. "I got an owie."

"I know. I'll be careful."

While Beau used a napkin to clean around the wound, he spoke to the mom, who'd turned pale to the lips as soon as he'd started mopping up the blood. "Mrs.?"

"Beth. I'm Beth."

"Hi, Beth. Do you have a compact or mirror in your purse?"

"A mirror? Um...yes. I do." She grabbed her purse from the back of her chair and dug through it. "Here," she held it out to him.

"Great. You hold on to that. Savannah?"

She was so lost in watching him work it took her a moment to realize he'd said her name. "Yes?"

"Meet Beth. Beth, this is my fr—my fiancée, Savannah. You've got some blood on your face and neck. Would you mind if Savannah scared up a glass of water and some more napkins to help you wash up?"

"Oh. Gosh. No." She glanced at Savannah. "I'd appreciate

it."

"No worries. I'll be right back." She'd barely taken a step when a waitress appeared and handed her a glass of water and several napkins. She crouched beside Beth, put the glass of water on the floor, and traded the napkins for Beth's small silver compact. She held the mirror and the other woman scrubbed off what she could. Beau kept up a low running commentary. "I see the cut. It's a little less than an inch long and about a quarter-inch deep."

"Goodness, it's much smaller than I imagined." Relief put a quaver in Beth's voice. "With all the blood, I thought laceration, skull fracture…I don't even know what I thought."

"Kids' heads have extra padding, but as a result they bleed a lot even from a relatively shallow cut. I can wrap him up well enough to hold him over while you drive to the ER. They can close the wound there."

"Thank you. Honestly, I'm so grateful." She accepted her compact back from Savannah with a weak smile.

"We're happy to help." Beau folded a fresh napkin into a strip. "Hey, Liam, do you like pirates?"

"Arrr!"

"Who's your favorite?"

"Jake. He always wins the treasure over Captain Hook."

"He's my favorite, too. And what does Jake wear around his head?"

"A red thing." He scrunched up his face. "I forget the word."

"Bandanna. Exactly. I'm going wrap this napkin around your head so you look just like Jake, okay? When I'm done you can check yourself out in your mom's mirror and tell me what you think."

Savannah bit her lower lip to keep it from trembling. This man tried so hard to remain detached, but he was the first to respond to a cry for help, and did so much more than simply evaluate and treat. He empathized. He cared. Her stupid heart wandered closer to a cliff she hadn't wanted to acknowledge lay ahead. A steep one that likely ended with a hard landing.

Liam sat still while Beau secured a clean napkin around his head, then handed the phone back to Beau and took the mirror from his mom. He turned his head right and left, checking himself out from every angle.

"Cool?" Beau asked.

"Cool."

"I think so, too. Now I need to ask you for a couple promises. Your mom is going to drive you to a place where people go to get their owies fixed and I need you to promise to leave the bandanna alone until a doctor or nurse takes it off. Got it?"

"I promise."

"Thanks. And when the doctor or nurse takes the bandanna off, they're going to do things to close up your owie and help it heal correctly. I want you to promise me you'll be brave like Jake, and let them do what they have to do."

"Uh-uh. I don't want them to touch it! That will hurt me a lot!"

Beau dipped his head and looked the upset boy in the eye. "I promise it won't hurt a lot." He lifted his hair away from his forehead and pointed to the thin row of black stitches visible at his hairline. "See this?"

Liam nodded.

"I got a bad owie on my head last week. I went to the doctor, too, and she used stitches to close the cut, so I know what I'm talking about when I say it doesn't hurt a lot."

"For real?"

"For real," Beau said, and helped the little boy to his feet. "Can I get a high five?" He held up his big, strong hand for a slap from Liam's miniature one, and Savannah's ovaries exploded. A little more of her emotional safe ground slipped out from under her.

"Thank you so much." Beth wrapped Beau in a hug, and then, to Savannah's surprise, she found herself the recipient of the same treatment.

The woman smiled as she drew away. "He's so good with kids. Hang on to him, honey. You've got yourself a keeper."

Chapter Fourteen

Beau ate the last handful of his french fries and watched his partner crumple his empty burger wrapper, toss it in the bag nestled in the console between them, and take a giant slug of his bladder-buster-sized soda. A second later Hunter let loose a thunderous belch, and then grinned proudly. "My compliments to the chef."

"Jesus Christ." Beau threw his wadded sandwich wrapper at Hunter, who batted it back at him. "You're a pig."

"I hate to break it to you, princess, but that burp is likely to be the least offensive thing to come out of me over the next half hour."

"Great." Beau hit the button to lower his window. "Hard to believe no lucky girl has scooped you up, what with all your charm."

Hunter gathered up the rest of the trash and dumped it in the bag. "I reserve some of my charm just for you, Beauregard. But speaking of lucky girls, how's your fiancée working out?"

"Fine."

"Better than fine, I'd hazard. Based on the goofy smile

stretching your ugly face these past few days, I assume you finally gave up your second virginity to your tasty little neighbor."

The second virginity comment irked, and Beau decided Hunt could handle the next puking drunk call they caught. "I don't kiss and tell."

"You do. You just don't know you do. Did you two sell it to your parents the other night?"

"Yeah. We sold it so well she got roped into going wedding dress shopping the week after my mom's surgery."

"Hmm." Hunter leaned back in his seat and smiled. "I picture her in something ivory and form-fitting."

"Stop picturing her in anything, dumbass. We're not getting married, remember?"

But it was all too easy to envision Savannah wrapped in curve-hugging satin. Just like it had been all too easy to ask her to spend the night after dinner with his parents, all too easy to fall into a habit of listening for her footsteps on the stairs, opening his door in invitation, and watching her accept with a slow, sexy smile. The easiest thing of all? Sinking into her warm, giving body, hearing her uncensored cries, and feeling her tremble as her eyes went blind and his name fell from her lips.

"The better question is do *you* remember? And does *she* remember?"

"We remember." True, he was batting a thousand every night with Savannah and they were both enjoying the hot streak, but this season would come to an end. Neither of them had lost sight of the fact.

A woman with a little girl about three or four years old walked down the sidewalk past the rig. The girl had long white-blonde curls just like Savannah's when she'd been that age. What was she doing right now?

"If you two are hitting it off so well, why not let things

ride and see where this goes? I know your families expect a wedding, but tell them you decided on a long engagement to…I don't know…save up for your dream wedding."

Hitting it off with Savannah had turned out to be easier than he'd imagined. He'd pegged her as loud and distracting when she'd first moved in—and he really hadn't known what to make of her being an artist except it sounded flighty and impractical—but she was also vibrant, funny, passionate, and incredibly *com*passionate. Whether critiquing their first kiss, punching her ex in the nose, or reading palms, she never failed to captivate, and as much as he'd balked about having her clutter spill over into his life, he was getting used to seeing her earrings sitting on his nightstand or her sweater tossed over the back of his sofa.

"She's leaving for nine months in Italy come the first of the year."

"So? I hear absence makes the heart grow fonder. Nine months of long-distance calls and Skype sex, then you're back to doing whatever you're doing now."

Sounded great, except that other than pretending to be engaged for the sake of his parents, he couldn't explain what they were doing now, and he sure as hell couldn't say where it led, other than far short of a place fair for Savannah. She wanted the whole deal—marriage, kids, happily ever after. She deserved a man who could give her all that and more. He was not that guy, and it was only a matter of time before she found some lucky bastard to step up and deliver.

"What we're doing works for now, but I don't have any more to offer. I'm played out when it comes to gambling on the future."

Hunter stared out the windshield for a moment, then turned, and Beau found himself on the receiving end of an uncharacteristically serious look from his partner. "You might want to reevaluate your hand before the first of the year. I don't know what the future holds, either, but I do know these last few days you've been happy. Happier than I've seen you in three long years."

. . .

Savannah hurried off the elevator and down the corridor to the surgi-center waiting area. She scanned the small, sparsely occupied lounge for Beau's dad, and almost started for the reception desk to ask if Cheryl Montgomery had come out of surgery when she spotted Beau sitting in the corner of the room. He wore jeans and a brown crew-neck sweater the same shade as his eyes, and looked big and restless with an arm slung across the back of the empty seat beside him and his right ankle resting on his bouncing left knee. He stared blankly at the television mounted on the wall beside the reception desk. A daytime soap played with the sound down.

Dark eyes moved her way when she approached. "Hey," she whispered and took the seat beside him. "Any news?"

His expression remained unreadable. He shifted, drawing himself in, resting his forearms on his thighs and linking his hands. The move effectively turned him into an island. As if he believed nobody would detect his anxiety so long as he maintained a perimeter.

"I thought we agreed you'd go to the meeting with the gallery today."

"I did go, but we wrapped up quickly. The showcase is on track so I popped over to see if your dad needed anything." She rubbed his tense shoulders, and then let her hand stray down his arm. Available if he wanted it. "What's your excuse?"

"I always come here on my days off, and"—he looked up at the TV—"watch my stories."

"Right. Because you don't have a TV at home."

"I don't like to watch the show alone. It's too intense." He unclenched his hands and took hold of hers. "The redhead there is a sociopathic man-eater."

She wove her fingers between his, gratified when he squeezed them. "You diagnosed all that with the sound down?"

"The acting stands on its own."

"I'll take your word. How's your mom?"

He leaned in and rested his forehead on her shoulder. His breath released in a long, shaky exhale. "She's good. The surgeon said the procedure went textbook, and lab results should be available by the end of the week. Mom's in recovery and Dad just went back to be the first thing she sees when she wakes up."

"That's sweet." She reached for his other hand and held it in hers. "I'm glad the surgery is over and everything went well."

"Me, too." He lifted their linked hands, ran his lips over her knuckles, and then raised his head and looked her square in the eyes. "Thanks for coming, Savannah."

God save her from this self-contained man. She'd have driven over with him if he'd asked her to, but he hadn't. Still, his appreciation eased the sting of his blatant reluctance to rely on her. "I couldn't stay away. You understand."

"Yeah, I do." He brought her hand to his lips again and kissed it. "Want to get out of here?"

"Whenever you're ready. If you prefer to stick around and see your mom?"

"No. She's in good hands, and I don't want to make her uncomfortable." He stood, pulled her to her feet, and started toward the elevator. "My dad's going to take her home. I'll call tonight and check in."

They rode the elevator in silence. He walked her to her car and paused by her door. "Feel like a late lunch?"

She shook her head. Not so much. And if she was reading

him right, neither did he.

"See you at home?"

She nodded and tried to ignore the reckless pirouette her heart executed at his use of the word "home."

On the drive *home* she attempted to talk sense into herself. By home, he probably meant Camden Gardens, but in truth she was starting to feel at home in his bed. They'd spent every night together since the evening at her studio, and each time she'd drifted off to sleep as breathless, boneless, and thoroughly satisfied as the first time. The inferno between them showed no sign of burning out. Her hormones insisted any sane, healthy woman would find herself addicted to rebound sex of this magnitude, but her better judgment kept harping on the danger of the addiction. It insisted getting hooked on devastating orgasms was problem enough, but getting accustomed to falling asleep with her head on his chest and his heartbeat thumping like a steady lullaby in her ear only invited heartache. She was already in deeper than she ought to be, and she'd begun to look at the first of the year with a weird combination of dread and relief.

The exact same combination of emotions churned in her stomach when she climbed out of her Explorer and saw Beau leaning against the wall by the stairwell, waiting for her. He straightened as she approached, took her hand, and said, "Can I buy you a drink?"

A peek at her watch told her it was barely two in the afternoon, but she suspected mentioning the time wouldn't dissuade him. Not that she blamed him for wanting to take the edge off. His mom's surgery had gone well, but now the stress of awaiting the lab results became all the more acute. This strong, independent, don't-rely-on-anyone man needed comfort and company. She could offer both. *And love*, a fatalistic inner voice acknowledged. *You've in love with this strong, independent, don't-rely-on-anyone man*. She couldn't pinpoint the moment when she'd lost the battle to keep her emotions on a safe path, but she had. She'd fallen, and there wasn't a thing in the world she could do to reverse course, even knowing he'd sooner cut out his heart than risk loving again. Hopefully her heart was more resilient. Hopefully she could be here for him while he needed her, and then find the strength to get on a plane and move on with her life. "Where did you have in mind for this drink?"

"I know just the place." He led her upstairs and into his apartment. "Make yourself comfortable. I'll find the bartender," he said and stepped into the kitchen.

While he dug around in the cabinet above the fridge, she pulled the ponytail holder out of her hair and tossed it on an end table. Next came the stack of silver "bamboo" bangles Sinclair had given her a few birthdays ago. Then she settled herself on the arm of the sofa and kicked off the Prada zipper-back black stilettos she'd treated herself to when she'd sold her first piece in Atlanta—shoes she should have waited to purchase until she'd collected her commissions. Her slightly punished toes forgave the fashionable torture as she massaged them through her black tights. After a moment she straightened, peeled out of her cropped leather motorcycle jacket, and tossed it across the back of the sofa.

The rustling in the kitchen ceased. She looked up to find Beau staring at her.

"What?" She got to her feet, and her hands automatically drifted over her long black knit dress, checking the turtleneck collar, straightening seams, smoothing the line of the skirt.

He shook his head and smiled. "Nothing. Just admiring how you come into a room."

The little trail of cast-offs around her drew her attention. In the course of three minutes she'd strewn more personal items into his living space than he kept there on a permanent basis. "Sorry. I'm not neat." She made her way into the kitchen.

"But I have other qualities."

His smiled tightened into a cocky grin. "I'm intimately familiar with your qualities."

She patted his cheek and gave him her own cocky grin. "You've only scratched the surface of my qualities." She'd never witnessed him drink anything stronger than beer, so she was a little surprised to see he'd lined up a nearly full bottle of tequila, a still-sealed bottle of vodka, and three-quarters of a bottle of whiskey. "You were serious about that drink."

"Any preference?"

"I prefer simple." She reached up and opened the long, narrow cabinet to the right of the sink, pulled out two short tumblers and placed them on the counter. Then she unscrewed the top from the bottle of Jack and poured two fingers in each glass.

After handing him one, she lifted the other and tapped it to his. "To your brave, strong, totally kick-ass mom."

"To Mom," he echoed, and downed his drink.

She did the same and refilled their glasses. "To your dad, who keeps her path smooth, in that laid-back, quiet way of his."

"To Dad." He knocked back the second shot. She followed suit.

The throat of the bottle tinkled against the rim of the glass as she refilled their tumblers. After putting the bottle aside she lifted her shot. "To you, for being there, even though it's scary. Even though she gave you an out because she's trying to protect you."

He downed the third shot without toasting, lowered his chin to his chest, and exhaled through his nose before replying. "I don't need protecting."

Those normally sharp brown eyes didn't quite lock on his glass, or her, or anything he looked at. "Of course you don't." She poured more Jack into their tumblers. "You're a big, strong, invincible guy. You can handle anything." She tipped her head toward the living room. "Want to sit down?"

"Sure." The word came out a little soft around the edges. Three shots in as many minutes had a noticeable effect on Mr. Invincible. She carried the bottle and her glass over to the coffee table and sank down on the sofa. He followed, and she noticed the little stumble and the way his lax body took an extra bounce when he plunked down beside her. He faced her and wound a stand of her hair around his finger while his eyes roamed her face. "You're beautiful."

"You're drunk."

"I'm getting there, but you're still beautiful." His eyes narrowed. "And sober."

She folded her legs under her and turned her body toward his. "Honey, the man I dated my last two years of college and all through grad school came from a family of whiskey distillers. Me and Tennessee do just fine."

He leaned forward, lifted the bottle off the table, and splashed some more in her glass. "Drink up."

"You think you can get me wasted? You'll pass out trying."

He raised one dark brow at her. "I've got body weight and dehydrogenase in my favor."

"Be that as it may, I can drink you under the table."

"Is that a challenge, Smith?"

"It's a fact, Montgomery." Just to prove her point, she picked up her glass and tossed back the shot. "Your turn." She poured another two fingers in his tumbler, handed it to him, and set the bottle aside. Enough alcohol. She had better ways to give him a temporary respite from the worry weighing on his mind. He downed the drink, those expressive lips twisting into a grimace as he swallowed.

"Now let's test your reflexes." She hiked the hem of her dress above her knees, slung one leg over his lap and straddled him. He grasped her hips as she arranged herself on his hard thighs.

When she stilled, he cradled her butt in his big hands and scooted her closer. "I passed," he said against the side of her throat.

She cupped his cheeks and drew his head back. "That wasn't the test. This is." She lowered her mouth to his and sank into a long, slow, whiskey-soaked kiss. His head tipped back against the sofa, and she thought for a moment he might let her have her way with him, but then long fingers tangled in her hair, and he leaned forward, changing the angle of the kiss. His reflexes were still pretty sharp, but hers were sharper. The knowledge sent a shiver along her spine. Beau tended to storm her senses, leave her shuddering, gasping, and utterly at his mercy, but this time the tables would turn. She reached down between their bodies, grabbed two handfuls of his sweater, and pulled it over his head.

"I love your chest," she said between kisses, and let her hands run all over the warm, smooth terrain, from the hard planes of his pecs to the channel between, which ran due south and provided a perfect path to guide her fingers down his abs. Her tongue tingled to follow the same route.

"Coincidentally, I feel the same about yours," he murmured, and drew her dress up. She raised her arms and let him peel it off, but shifted away when he leaned close and reached for the back clasp of her bra.

"Uh-uh. Keep those hands to yourself. I'm not finished testing your reflexes." She ran her fingertips over the ridges of muscle bracketing his abs, all the way to where they disappeared beneath the waistband of his jeans.

"Savannah." His low voice vibrated with warning.

"Yes, Beau?" She traced the edge of his waistband until her fingers arrived at his fly. The bulge straining the line of buttons there jumped under the brush of her hand, but his fingers intercepted hers.

"Four shots of whiskey have an effect on a man's reflexes."

"I'll be the judge." She wiggled her fingers out of his grasp and went back to work on his fly.

"No you won't. I made you a firm promise a while back. You get nothing short of my best every single time I'm inside you, or…Jesus that feels good."

She swept her thumb again over the smooth head peeking from the waistband of his underwear, this time lingering longer to explore the small opening at the center. He groaned and flexed his hips.

"See, you've got excellent reflexes." She slipped off his lap and onto her knees, parted his jeans, and freed him the rest of the way from his boxer briefs. He raised his head and their eyes met. While he watched, she traced a fingertip along the length of his shaft.

"They're improving by the second, but—"

"Just one last test." The big, strong, invincible man she loved needed an escape, and she could provide one. Leaning in, she kissed the very tip of his erection. "Don't worry, it's painless."

Despite her promise, when she parted her lips and slowly took him into her mouth, she wrung a low, tortured curse out of him. "Fuck it, Savannah. You're killing me."

She reversed course, appreciating the hitch in his breath, and then paused to look at him. "But you'll die with a smile on your face."

"You're determined to take me down, huh?"

"Mmm-hmm." She let the response vibrate around him, loving how his eyelids suddenly struggled with gravity, and flags of color unfurled across his cheekbones. A large hand cupped the back of her head, guiding her, but not usurping control.

When she dug into his jeans and cupped his balls, he murmured her name.

"Hmm?" Oh yeah, he liked that. The hand on her head tightened.

"It's not going to take long."

She laved the smooth crown, and then speared the tip of her tongue into the opening. At the same time, she gave his balls a pump. His big body jerked, and a fast, harsh inhale reached her ears.

"Okay. I'm there. You should stop before I—"

"Beau?" She had to raise her head to speak, but she refused to relinquish her grip on the boys.

"What?" His tortured reply pleased her almost as much as the desperate look in his eyes.

"Sit back, relax, and let me take care of you." Before he could respond, she lowered her head and encased him, taking him in as deep as she could without denying herself oxygen. Then she squeezed again.

The hand in her hair fisted. Muscles tensed, and then long, hard-fought words echoed in her ears as she drained him. "Jesus. Savannah. I *love* the way you take care of me."

Her heart trembled.

No, but you would. You would if you'd really let me.

Chapter Fifteen

"I get nervous when you do that, Smith."

"What? This?" Naturally, she kept right at it.

Beau tightened his grip on the steering wheel and forced his attention back to the road. "Yes. That. Do you have any idea how many accidents I see involving exactly what you're doing right now?"

She shrugged. "Then you'd really hate watching me do it while *I'm* driving."

Good point. "At least give it a rest while I make this turn."

"Oh, please. I've done this while going over railroad tracks—at forty miles per hour—without a single mishap."

Before he could give her shit about taking railroad tracks at forty miles an hour, she lowered her hand from her face and waited while he steered the Yukon into the parking lot of the Chattahoochee Tavern. As soon as he slid into one of the few remaining open slots, she flicked on the interior light and resumed applying black gunk to her eyelashes with a long, potentially blinding wand. What was the female preoccupation with eyelashes, anyway? He supposed he'd notice if someone didn't have any, but short of that...

She tossed the tube into her oversize red purse and dug around for something else.

"You don't need the war paint. You look beautiful."

"I look like I haven't seen a ray of sun in almost a week — which I haven't." Her attention never wavered from the bag. "I need blush."

He crossed his arms and settled into the seat. "I could make you blush."

She arched her brows at him. "And mess up all my hard work? I'd have to start all over again. But it's nice to know someone's ready to have fun this evening."

He was. For the first time in a long time he actually looked forward to a holiday party. Some credit went to his mom, who'd called that morning to tell him her pathology results couldn't have been better. Clear margins, clear nodes. She'd passed the news along to him as casually as discussing the weather, and then dived right into plans for when he and Savannah visited, but he'd been a little too distracted by the waves of relief washing over him to pay much attention.

Hell yeah, he was ready to have some fun.

Savannah took a break from moving a fat brush over her cheeks in rapid circles. "That makes two of us. I'm really happy to know your mom is in the clear."

"Me, too."

She smiled, and then tipped her head toward the mirror again and slicked some glossy red stuff on her lips. The way she held her lips open and moved the wand over them sent his memory sliding back to the other night, on his sofa, and the feel of those soft but nimble lips cradling his highly appreciative cock.

When she finished, she dropped the gloss in her bag and turned to him. He flicked off the dome light, which left the interior of the car gilded by the soft white glow from the lights around the tavern's parking lot. He turned to her, propped his left arm on the steering wheel, and leaned closer. Hemmed her in when it came right down to it, but he didn't think she'd mind. "Tell me, Savannah, do you have everything you need in that bag of yours to redo all this?" He ran his finger along her cheekbone.

Long, darkened lashes fluttered, and his groin tightened. Maybe he was a lash man after all?

"Why would I need to redo it?"

He cupped her jaw, tipping her face up, and brought his mouth inches from hers. Her gleaming lips parted. "Because I'm about to mess you—"

A thump on the driver's side window brought them both up short. He craned his neck to find Hunter's grinning face on the other side of the glass.

"Go away."

"You want privacy? Seriously? You're in a fucking parking lot, Lancelot. Anyway, Ashley wants to meet your fiancée. Or as she put it, she wants proof of life."

His partner reached out and snagged someone by the arm, and a second later Ashley's exasperated face appeared at his window. "I did not say that."

Beau lowered his window. "Hi, Ash. Did you two come together?"

"Absolutely not," she replied. "I was walking in. He was walking in. I didn't walk fast enough."

"She's lying. She deliberately fiddled with her shoe just to make sure I caught up."

"I stepped in a pothole."

"On purpose."

"I'm three seconds from kneeing you in the balls. On purpose."

"Merry Christmas to you, too, Ash."

Rather than watch his partner take one in the family

jewels, Beau opened his door and looked back at Savannah. "They're harmless. I promise."

She laughed and opened her door. "I'm not worried."

Hunter rounded the front of the truck and offered her a hand. "Hi, Savannah. Pleasure to officially meet you."

"Likewise."

He gestured to Ashley. "This ball-buster is Ashley... Ow!"

The brunette lifted the skinny heel of her red leather ankle boot from Hunter's instep and shook Savannah's hand. "Congratulations on your engagement."

"Thank you."

"I've worked with these two for a long time, and I have a soft spot for one of them," Ashley said.

"You have a funny way of showing it," Hunter complained.

"Not you." She patted Beau on the shoulder. "You. Though I have to admit, he's given me some moments over the years."

Savannah glanced at him. "You don't say?"

"I do. The stories I could tell. One of these days we'll have to grab a drink and I'll give you the lowdown."

Savannah fell into step beside Ashley. "Oh, look. A tavern. Can I buy you a drink?"

Beau held the door while Savannah and Ashley chatted their way into the bar. "Bet she's talking about the time you passed out giving twenty-five kindergartners a tour of the station," Hunter said as he walked in.

"I'm not going to take that bet. I am going to take a beer, and"—he stepped away for a minute to confer with the ladies—"Savannah wants a white wine, and Ashley wants champagne. You might as well run a tab."

"And I'm buying because?"

"Because I remember who blurted the news about my *engagement*, thus giving Ashley the opportunity to spend an evening assassinating my character."

Hunter rolled his eyes. "Whatever. But I'm not a cocktail waitress. Come with me."

Somehow he ended up buying the drinks while Hunter played barmaid, and then got cornered by the deputy chief of operations, who wanted to talk shop. Hunter and a couple of intermediates joined in. Beau propped his back against the bar and nursed his beer, keeping one ear in the conversation while he watched Savannah circulate around the room as Ashley introduced her to other members of the team. In a sea of soft lights and indistinct bodies, she glowed, like his personal beacon.

Safe harbor. The thought sprang out of nowhere, and spiked his pulse because he knew better. Yes, she was beautiful, smart, and funny. On top of all that, she possessed bone-deep compassion and instinctive generosity. If he let himself, he could fall hard for her.

Don't let yourself, because you're not the kind of man who can risk another fall. She's leaving in a few weeks. Even if she weren't, there are no safe harbors for you, and forgetting that is the most dangerous thing you can do.

Still, he couldn't tear his eyes away from her.

Converted gas lanterns overhead put a copper halo around her long, loose hair. She smiled, and laughed, and shook a dozen hands, but every so often those smoky eyes found their way back to him, and her polite, social smile turned into something else. Something that said, *After this, let's head back to your place and have a party for two.*

Just like that, the anxiety subsided. *This* was the safe harbor. Their physical connection he could handle, no matter how urgent or overriding it might feel. He knew exactly how to satisfy those needs. His lips automatically stretched into an answering smile made of *Hell, yes.*

The deputy chief congratulated him on his engagement, and he forced his attention back to the men in front of him and said, "Thanks." Then the older man pinned Hunter with a sharp look and asked when *he* planned to settle down. Beau patted his partner on the back and excused himself, ignoring Hunter's silent plea for rescue.

He figured he'd have to track Savannah down, but when he turned, he nearly stumbled into her.

Her hands clasped his shoulders for balance, and then lingered, palms sliding down the front of the soft, light gray crew neck he'd worn specifically to entice her touch. Mission accomplished. He drew her in close. "Thanks for doing this. Socializing with my coworkers goes above and beyond the call of duty."

She eased back and sent him her lopsided grin. "Are you kidding? Where else would I have learned about the time you neglected to secure the back doors of the ambulance, drove off, and dumped the gurney in the middle of the street?"

Assholes. "In my defense, I'll mention the street was actually a driveway, the gurney was empty, and the doors on that rig never latched correctly."

"Especially when you don't shut them properly—so I hear," she added when he glared at her.

"You can't believe everything you hear. Not out of this crew."

She bit her lip to keep from smiling, and the small gesture made him want to haul her back to the car, drive home, and spend the next several hours making her bite her lip to keep from screaming things like, "Oh, God. Right there. Yes. Yes. Yes," at the top of her lungs. Manners probably dictated they hang out another ten minutes—fuck it, five minutes—just to be civilized. "Did you have your check-in with the gallery today?"

"I did." Those bright blue eyes dimmed a little.

"And?"

"It went well. In fact, the manager told me if I weren't

going to Italy they'd sign me to an extended deal. Not just for the works I'm exhibiting at the showcase, but everything I produced over the next year."

If I weren't going to Italy. He liked the suggestion more than he ought to, especially because her departure represented their ideal exit strategy. "Why can't you do both?"

"The fellowship is designed to support and foster undiscovered artists, not those actively promoted by a major gallery. Signing with Mercer to participate in the New Year's Eve spotlight and exhibit a handful of pieces doesn't qualify as being 'actively promoted,' but if I entered into a commission agreement of the scope Mercer's proposing, I would meet the definition."

"Could you defer the fellowship for a year, and see how things worked out with Mercer?"

She chewed her lip. "I could request a deferral. The foundation grants them from time to time, but I doubt they'd extend the courtesy on the basis of me wanting to see how my career worked out with a gallery that is, technically, a competitor."

"I guess this comes down to one important question. How badly do you want to see Venice?" He meant the question as a joke, but his gut tensed.

"Ha. I spent a semester abroad during my MFA studying glassmaking techniques in Europe, so I've seen Venice. Lovely city, but location isn't the primary draw. The fellowship offers a sure thing for the next nine months, which means a lot to me after the instability of the last few. It's also a chance to reboot my career. I give up some autonomy, but the foundation features my work and presents me to a whole new level of collectors and buyers. Not a guarantee, of course, but a chance. "

"Too good a chance to pass up?"

"Probably." The little crinkle appeared between her

brows, and he wanted to kiss it away. "I applied for the fellowship because my career here stalled. Hell, it tanked. But my pride hates to see me abandon Atlanta as a failure, even for something as coveted as the Solomon Foundation. Maybe the Mercer Gallery offer means I should stay the course?"

"What do you *want* to do, Savannah?"

Do you really want to know the answer? So what if she does want to stay? That's a career decision. It doesn't mean she intends to waste more time in a dead-end …whatever…you can't even call it a relationship, with a man who can't offer her the kind of future she deserves.

She stared at him for a long moment, opened her mouth to speak, but then shook her head. "What I want for the future is too big a question for me to answer right now." Her fingers danced over the back of his neck and sank into his hair. "Ask me what I want to do for the rest of the night."

The world straightened. The ground under his feet solidified. "You think you've got the whole night in you, Smith? Because I guarantee I do."

Her lips curved. "I'm counting on it, Montgomery."

• • •

"Damn, you're gorgeous. Delicate, but powerful. Graceful, yet undeniably sexy. I can't wait to get inside you."

Savannah stood in her strapless bra and matching thong, and let her hands roam, exploring every line and contour, luxuriating in every breathtaking detail…until a knock on the other side of the door interrupted the seduction. A polite female voice called, "Do you need any assistance?"

"No, no. I'm good. I'll be out in a minute." She cast a nervous glance at the door and then turned back to the object of her lust. "Okay, let's do this. I promise I'll be gentle."

The sleek column of ivory satin seeded with tiny

Swarovski crystals seemed to wink at her. She lowered the side zipper and then lifted the dress off the hanger. The $3,000 price tag mandated she be very, very gentle. Frankly, she had no business even trying the thing on. She didn't need a wedding dress, much less a $3,000 one, but the moms had been so excited about the shopping trip—they'd even dragged poor Sinclair along as the designated driver—and after a few complimentary glasses of champagne at the bridal boutique, she'd gotten kind of swept up in the moment. When the sales associate had smiled and said, "This is a smidge beyond the budget you mentioned, but I think it would be perfect," Savannah hadn't had the strength to resist. What harm could come from trying it on?

Stepping into the cool, silk embrace sent a decadent shiver along her spine. She zipped herself in and turned to look at her reflection in the full-length fitting room mirror. The gown might as well have been made for her. Aside from the length—everything she tried on was miles too long—the dress hugged her body like an opulent second skin, and flared out above her knees in a dramatic sweep of skirt. The strapless sweetheart neckline left her shoulders bare and presented an unapologetically feminine silhouette. She could wear her hair up, and maybe Sinclair could design a necklace to... *Holy shit, Savannah, reel it in. You're not getting married.*

"How're we doing in there?"

We're trying on a dress I'd have to sell a kidney to afford, for a wedding that's never going to happen. "Good."

"Your mother, sister, and future mother-in-law are dying to see the gown on you," the sales associate prompted. "Should I start the drum roll?"

"Sure." She took a deep breath, pasted a smile on her face, and opened the door. The sales associate's eyes moved over her in quick assessment.

"Go on out and step up on the riser. I'm going to grab

my hem clips. Y'all are going to want to see the way this will actually look on the big day."

Guilt stabbed Savannah as she walked to the main room of the boutique where her entourage sat chatting. The salesclerk clearly thought she was going to say yes to the dress. The willowy brunette was probably already mentally spending her commission check...hopefully not on shoes for her five fatherless children.

Three sets of eyes turned to her, and conversation stopped. After a beat or two of being silently stared at, she started to feel self-conscious. "This one's pretty, but maybe a little too...too?"

Mrs. Montgomery let out one warning sniffle, and then dissolved into tears.

All of a sudden Savannah realized Beau's mom had been through this ritual before. "Oh my God. I'm sorry. Is this stirring up painful memories?"

"No," the older woman assured her between sobs. "Kelli's dress was completely different, and perfect for her, but this dress...Savannah, this gown is perfect for *you*." She offered up a watery smile. "I can't wait to see Beau's reaction."

Yeah. That will be interesting.

"You look lovely," her mom agreed as she took a couple of tissues from the box the sales associate offered, and mopped her damp cheeks. "That is definitely the one."

"You guys need to take it easy on the champagne."

The saleslady knelt at the base of the riser and began clipping the hem at the front of the dress to the appropriate length. "Don't think it's just the champagne talking. The dress really does flatter you. I've developed sort of an eye for matching the gown to the girl."

Guilt prickled again. Time for some honesty. "You absolutely have." She ran her hand down the rich fabric and sighed. "I love this dress. It's straight out of my dreams. And way out of my price range."

"I wouldn't be much good at matching the gown to the girl if I didn't factor in the budget." She stood and winked at Savannah. "Your mother and future mother-in-law have a surprise for you."

Uh-oh.

"Cheryl and I are going splitzies on the dress," her mother announced, beaming.

Savannah turned to Sinclair and caught her in the act of wiping her brimming eyes.

"What? It wasn't my idea."

No, she had a pretty good idea the moms came up with the gesture themselves, but her sister was sitting there, enabling all the same. "Stop crying. You haven't had any champagne."

"Can I help if I'm a sucker for a perfect wedding dress?"

"But you *know* we shouldn't rush to a decision," Savannah insisted and sent her sister the best *Help me!* stare she could manage.

Sinclair lifted one slim shoulder and let it drop. "You love the dress. It's straight out of your dreams. What reason do I have for suggesting we sleep on it?"

She could think of three thousand reasons, but she couldn't utter a single one.

"Please, Savannah, let your mother and me do this. You don't know what it means to me to see Beau take another chance at love, marriage—sharing his life with someone. What happened with Kelli and Abbey shook his faith in everything, including himself. Trent and I feared he'd never open himself up to love again."

Mercy, what could she say? "His ability to love so intensely is part of what makes him so amazing."

"He does love intensely. I see the intensity when he's with you. He reaches for you. He seeks comfort from you. He lets you in. You're good for him, and he's needed something good for a long time. We all have."

Savannah sank into the empty chair on the other side of her mom. Condolences leaped to her tongue, but she held them back because she noticed Mrs. Montgomery's voice remained stable and her eyes dry. This woman would burst into tears at the first hint of joyful news, but she'd learned to be strong in the face of adversity. She'd learned to be strong for her son.

Her heart broke for them all over again. "I can't imagine how awful it was, for all of you."

Cheryl nodded. "I don't wish the experience on anyone, but I do wish I'd handled it differently."

"You were there for him—"

"No, we were there *with* him, but not really for him. Trent and I allowed our grief to distract us from a troubling reality. Beau coped with his pain, and his profound sense of helplessness, by emotionally withdrawing from everyone. He took the same detachment he relies on to do his job effectively and applied it to all aspects of his life. Oh, he went through the motions of interacting, and maintaining relationships to a degree—a very superficial degree—but he wasn't truly connecting anymore. We told ourselves to be patient. He'd let people back into his life when his heart healed. We also made excuses. Trent and I told each other, 'It's only been a year. Give him time.' A year stretched into two, and then three, and we started to fear he'd never take down the wall he'd constructed around himself. And then suddenly he did, and we have you to thank."

No words could express how badly Savannah wished the sentiments were true, but they weren't. He still had the wall, and all she'd done was help him camouflage the barrier so the people who cared about him wouldn't detect it. She stared at the floor because she couldn't look anyone in the eye. "Please, don't thank me. He loves you." At least she could say that much honestly. This whole stupid deception arose out of his love for his parents and his desire to ease their concern. "Your patience and love made him realize he couldn't lock his feelings away. Trust me, what Beau and I have wouldn't exist if not for you."

"You have it, and that's what's important," her mom insisted. "Fate's full of surprises, and some of them are happy ones. When the happy surprises come along, we grab on to them, and we celebrate." She turned to the saleswoman and handed over her credit card. "We'll take the dress."

Sinclair gave Savannah a *told-you-so* look and Savannah recalled her sister's prediction. *You and Beau are going to end up married through the sheer force of Mom's will.*

Cheryl sniffled. "Beau's going to lose his mind when he sees you in that gown."

Savannah and Sinclair responded at the same time.

"No doubt."

Chapter Sixteen

The laughter echoing in the stairwell gave them away. Beau opened his door and stepped into the hall in time to see four tipsy women meander up the stairs, pausing every few steps to talk over one another and then dissolve into fits of giggles. His mom and Laurel had their arms looped around Savannah. Sinclair brought up the rear. Laurel leaned across Savannah and in a loud whisper said to his mom, "Now I just need to find someone for Sinclair, and then I can sit back and wait for grandbabies."

Sinclair sighed, gave him a pointed look, and checked her watch.

Correction. Three tipsy women and one sober one—though he doubted Sinclair would stay that way for long after her designated driver duties ended. She herded everyone to the landing. Savannah looked up at him with wide, owlish eyes and hung back.

Hmm.

The moms spotted him. His called out, "There's my boy!" The next thing he knew he was the recipient of two sloppy, unsteady mom hugs.

"Hey"—he caught each woman in an arm and supported them—"seems like you all had fun."

Sinclair rolled her eyes and peeled the moms off him. "'Fun' is not the word. These two are mine. This one's yours." She nudged Savannah his way. "She's hammered."

He tucked Savannah under his arm and looked down at her. "Really?"

She nodded. "Lil' bit."

She smelled like tequila and…tequila. He knew she could handle her whiskey. How much tequila did it take to get her drunk?

"We went out to dinner, to celebrate," his mom chimed in. "We found the perfect—"

"Shhh." Savannah put a finger to her lips. "Secret, remember?"

"Oh, that's right. I'm not supposed to tell him we picked out the perfect dress."

Laurel burst out laughing, staggered into his mom, and hung on. "You're like a vault, Cheryl."

He turned to Savannah, who winced and evaded his gaze. "You picked out a dress? As in, bought it…already?" he added when he realized his incredulous tone sounded odd for a supposedly engaged man.

"Not *a* dress," his mom scoffed. "*The* dress. You're going to love it—and such a steal at just three thousand dollars."

"Three thousand…" He couldn't finish the figure. Speech failed him.

Savannah slumped against him and moaned. "I think I'm going to be sick."

Him, too. But now he understood why she'd resorted to the Jose Cuervo. Clearly the afternoon of dress shopping had gone off the rails. "I think everyone's had enough excitement for one afternoon. Let's go inside and have some coffee." He swept her into his arms. She draped her hands around his neck and buried her face against the side of his throat.

"Sorry."

No, that should have been his line. He'd dragged her into this. He kissed her sweaty forehead. "Everything's okay, Smith. I've got you."

The moms sighed in unison, and then his said, "Remember the time Savannah fell off Beau's scooter and skinned her knee, and he carried her home?"

Savannah's mom nodded. "I always knew these two were destined to be together."

"On second thought, this might require a *lot* of coffee," he muttered, and led the way into his apartment.

"I'll make it," Sinclair offered, and walked over to the machine sitting on his kitchen counter.

He set Savannah on the sofa and eased one tall red heel off her foot. "Cabinet above the machine." He slid the other heel off, rotated her ankle in a slow circle, and smiled at her appreciative moan.

"Got it," Sinclair called from the kitchen.

Savannah's mom grabbed a magazine from the coffee table, sat down beside her daughter, and fanned her. "How're you doing, honey?"

She leaned back and her eyelids drooped to half mast. "Good. No." She straightened. "Not good." Then she leaped to her feet, scrambled around him, and hurried down the hall.

"Oh dear," his mom said. "Poor Savannah. What a way to end such a wonderful day."

Laurel stood, weaving a bit on her feet. "I better check on her."

He gestured Savannah's mom back to her seat. "Sit. I'll take care of her."

A short trip down the hall and through his bedroom brought him to the closed bathroom door. He knocked once and then walked in. Savannah sat on the tile floor, her back propped against the tub, arms resting on her drawn-up knees. She raised her head and gave him a terrified look. "Three thousand dollars."

He hunkered down next to her and gathered her up onto his lap. "Don't panic." He stroked her hair and tried for a joke. "We'll return it when they're not looking."

Sinclair appeared at the door and handed him a bottle of water. "Nope."

He took the bottle and offered it to Savannah. "Hydrate." Then he looked up at Sinclair. "What do you mean, 'Nope'?"

"Dresses need altering. They've already done the first cuts." She leaned against the doorframe and crossed her arms. "That sucker is nonreturnable."

Okay, it took a moment to choke the news down, but he managed. "That is…unfortunate, but don't worry, I'll pay for it."

A combination of a sob and a hiccup erupted from the woman on his lap. "T-that's not the w-worst part."

There was worse? He glanced at Sinclair. "It's an ugly dress?"

"Gorgeous dress. She's upset because the moms paid for it, as a wedding gift. There was no talking them out of it."

Aw, fuck. This wasn't about the damn dress. She was crumbling under guilt.

She sobbed harder, her tears soaking through his shirt, and now guilt—and something else he refused to name— formed an uncomfortable weight in his stomach. "Don't cry. Please. There's nothing for you to feel bad about. You haven't done anything wrong."

"I'm lying to our families. I'm a big lying liar."

He pulled a towel off the rack above their heads, tipped her face up, and dried her tears. "You're helping me heal my relationship with my parents, and you don't deserve to spend a second feeling conflicted about it. What you're doing means a lot to me." He tightened his hold on her. "*You* mean a lot to me." A flood of words gathered in his throat, but he swallowed them. He had a bad feeling what spilled out would break their "no complications" rule beyond repair.

As if it already isn't, for you. You shattered the rule the first time you kissed her, and letting her go will feel like ripping open a wound you never should have left vulnerable in the first place.

The only thing he could avoid at this point was inflicting any wounds on her. "Any fallout from this is on me, understand?"

Sinclair coughed. He'd been so intent on easing Savannah's conscience he'd forgotten she still stood there. "I'm going to go check on the moms," she said quietly. "Give you two a chance to talk."

He was racking up all kinds of debts to the Smith sisters. "Thanks."

Savannah sniffed and rubbed her eyes. "We'll be out in five."

"Take your time," she said, and shut the door behind her.

• • •

"How are you feeling?"

Savannah opened her eyes and stared into Beau's. They'd said goodbye to their moms and Sinclair, and she'd wandered back to his bedroom and flopped across the bed while he'd washed up the coffee mugs. No leaving dishes until tomorrow for him.

"I'm okay." Between washing her face, brushing her teeth, and downing two painkillers and a bottle of water, she felt almost human. The soft light from the bedside lamp didn't hurt, either. She reached up and brushed her fingers through his hair. "Sorry about tonight. I don't know what's wrong with me. I got stressed, and I didn't handle it well."

He gave her a quick smile and then flexed his arms and slowly lowered his body to hers. "Trust me, Smith. I'd be stressed to the breaking point if I spent the day dress shopping with our moms. Lucky for you"—he paused and bestowed a gentle kiss at her temple—"I know a foolproof"—another pause, another kiss on the opposite temple—"stress reliever."

God, she was easy. She raised her chin and parted her lips, already anticipating the pressure of his mouth on hers. Instead he lifted himself off her. Before she could utter a word of protest, he swept her red sweater over her head and flipped her around so she lay facedown on the mattress.

"Um"—she popped her head up—"I'm not so sure this constitutes a foolproof stress relieverrrrr…" Her words trailed off as big, warm hands moved her hair out of the way and went to work on the sore spot where her neck met her shoulders. "Never mind." Her muscles dissolved and her forehead hit the mattress. "I was wrong."

"Too hard? Too soft?"

"No, no." Those magic hands moved to her shoulders, and she bit back a moan. Sort of. "Just right."

"Then relax." He leaned in and his words feathered over her skin. "I told you I'd take care of you."

His palms slid down her back, along either side of her spine. Every sweep of his thumbs released tension she hadn't even realized her body held. Even her head felt better. He wrung the aches out like water from a sponge. When his thumbs found the dimples bracketing the base of her spine and pressed firmly, she groaned with relief.

Warm lips brushed the small of her back. Heat flowed in to replace the pain, and even though it felt like heaven, she raised herself onto her elbows and tried to roll away. Heat she could handle. There'd been heat between them from the very start. But this—his hands and mouth moving over her with tender yet erotic touches—made it too easy for her to feel cherished. Cared for. Loved. He made it too easy to let her soft heart hope for things she knew damn well he didn't want to offer. Case in point? The debate she'd been having with herself about passing on the fellowship and accepting the offer from the gallery. How much of her indecision stemmed from her desire to stay right here, in his arms, enjoying moments like this?

Too much.

His hand at the center of her back stopped her roll. "Did I hit a sore spot?"

"No." She blew her hair out of her face. "You hit all the right spots. No need for the seduction. I'm good to go."

He settled her against the bed again and trapped her hips between his knees. "What part of 'I'll take care of you' did you not understand?"

"The part where I had to lie here with a bad case of lady blue balls while you sat on me?"

He laughed, but only moved to shift himself lower. "Now you know. Shut up and let me finish my job."

She shut up, closed her eyes, and somehow endured as he trailed his mouth up her spine, using his tongue to trace every single vertebra. The whiskers on his cheeks and jaw tickled her skin, and she nearly squirmed. Quick fingers unclasped her bra and then teased the sides of her breasts while he nibbled her shoulder.

When he slid his hands under her and cupped her breasts, she sank her fingers into the bedspread and tried not to beg.

"Still good to go?"

She didn't trust her voice, so she nodded.

He rolled her over, and his eyes locked on hers. Slowly, purposefully, they slid down her body. His fingertips followed, gliding along her throat before trailing down her arms to draw the bra off. He popped the button on her jeans. The rasp of her zipper filled the room, and then he stood and tugged her jeans and underwear off.

Next came his shirt, and if he hadn't already rendered her speechless, the sight of shadows and light playing over every hard-etched curve and angle of chest and abs would have done the trick. She folded her arms behind her head and waited for him to remove his jeans. He unbuttoned the fly, but didn't take them off. Instead he knelt between her parted legs and kissed the inside of her knee. The scrape of whiskers contrasted with the soft kiss, and everything north of his lips started to tingle.

She levered herself up onto her elbows. "I appreciate the effort you're putting in here, but it's not necessary. I believe I mentioned my condition?"

He kissed the other leg, a little higher, and then deliberately ran his chin along her thigh until she shivered. "The lady blue balls?"

"Yep."

"I've got the cure." He moved to the other side and kissed her again, very high. She dropped back onto the mattress and sank a hand into his hair.

"I might not survive your cure."

His laugh tickled her skin, and then he hitched her legs into his arms and forced them wider. "You're safe with me."

She braced for what came next, anticipating his hot mouth, his lips, teeth, and tongue driving her straight into a fast, hard orgasm. But he lied. She wasn't safe at all, because he lowered his head and danced his tongue over her. Slowly, leisurely, as if he had all the time in the world and nothing more important to do than savor every second it took to reduce her to a trembling mass of need.

She tightened her fingers in his hair—probably too tight, but the urgency didn't allow for manners. "Oh God."

He came back for another pass. Her body tensed. Nerve endings caught fire. She blindly chased his tongue, which only made him tighten his hold to keep her hips still.

"Let me take care of you." His plea caressed her, as torturously light as his touch. Then his lips closed over the part of her most in need of care and bestowed a featherlight kiss. Followed by another, and another. She rocked into him, as much as his hold on her hips would permit, while the need built into something crushing.

"Beau," she breathed, but he didn't increase the pressure or the pace, just kept driving her insane with those slow, unbearably gentle kisses. Even the smallest move of his jaw brought his whiskers into contact with oversensitized flesh, to the point she literally itched for more.

Did he understand what he was doing to her? He slid a hand up her body, over her stomach, her torso, to come to rest between her breasts. On either side of his wide hand, her nipples throbbed in time to the slow, steady pull of his lips between her legs. She closed her eyes and waited for him to touch the aching peaks. It took several seconds before she realized he wasn't going to. No, he expected her to come like that, with his hand on her heart and his mouth slowly, patiently drawing the orgasm out of her.

"I can't. I can't…"

She sucked in a breath for a third denial, and that's when he proved her wrong. She could. She did, with devastating intensity. All the more devastating because he stayed with her, using increasingly light strokes to prolong every wave of pleasure. When he finally eased away, even she couldn't identify the sound that came out of her—some kind of moan.

Eventually she found her powers of speech. And her manners. "Thank you."

"Premature. I'm not done."

His words had her opening her eyes in time to see him

drag his jeans off. He stood there for a moment, like some living, breathing masterpiece of masculine power and beauty, and every sated inch of her suddenly hungered for more. For *him*.

He leaned over her and kissed her stomach, her heart, and then slid his arm around her waist and hauled her up until he had her stretched out across the bed. The hot, hard weight of his erection branded her thigh. His mouth grazed hers. Retreated. Came back for another brief kiss.

This man was going to wreck her. She wrapped her arms around his head and pulled him in, fused her mouth to his. He braced himself on his forearms and gave her what she silently demanded. The pressure of his mouth forced hers open wider. He took full advantage, delving deep, laying claim. His tongue filled her mouth, and left her desperately aware of a frustratingly empty part of her. She raised her knees and fluttered her thighs against his hips, not caring if she came across as impatient. The move nudged the smooth, wide head of his cock closer to the target, and her inner muscles quivered.

He extended his arms, breaking the kiss as he levered his upper body above hers. Her hands slid down to the small of his back. She blinked her eyes open and looked up at him.

"Still good to go, Savannah?"

She parted her thighs wider, opened herself for the first deep, driving thrust. "Go."

Except apparently tonight he preferred to torture her slowly. He sank into her inch by inch. She flattened her palms against his ass, urging him down, but he wouldn't be rushed. The angle of his hips pinned hers to the bed, thwarting any decent effort she might make to hurry him along. His shoulders shook. Sweat dampened the hair at his temples, but still he took his sweet time. His eyes never left her face.

"How long can you keep this up?"

A muscle twitched in his jaw, but still he managed a tight grin. "As long as it takes."

Her reply ended up being an inarticulate moan because he finally, finally settled in deep enough she could tighten her hips and get a brutally solid grind against the base of his cock. Her eyes nearly rolled back in her head. She made it last as long as she could, then moaned again as he slowly withdrew. And withdrew. And kept on withdrawing.

"No. No. No. No." She dug her fingernails into his ass and clamped her legs around his waist in an attempt to keep him.

He eased all the way out, and she didn't know whether to burst into tears or slug him. Or both.

"I love...being. Inside. You." He pushed into her again, a little more with each word, and the wet glide of his entry echoed in the room. "So much, I needed to feel that again, but you don't have to worry, Savannah. I will never leave you hanging. I will always"—thrust—"always"—thrust—"take care of you."

And now she really was blinking back tears, because terms like "never leave" and "always" weren't really in his vocabulary. Hearing them from him, even in this capacity, overwhelmed her. She turned away so he wouldn't see how his words affected her.

Movement to her right caught her attention. Her gaze homed in on the flat screen of the TV on the wall opposite the bed. The dark rectangle acted like a mirror, reflecting them. The knot of desire at her center twisted tighter as she watched the rippling muscles in Beau's shoulders, the slope of his back, the unspeakably sexy way his glutes bunched and relaxed with every unhurried thrust.

She couldn't tear her eyes away. He rocked into her, once, twice, and then moved his hips in a lazy circle, stirring her, hitting every trigger point along the way. He stilled. She whimpered.

"I'm glad you're enjoying the view, but"—callused fingers smoothed over her cheek and turned her face back to him—"look here now."

She didn't have much choice, but finding herself the focus of his dark, miss-no-detail eyes left her more exposed than she could afford. All she had left was her Southern sass, so she used it. "You're kind of strict about the eye contact, Beauregard."

He smiled, but didn't release her gaze. Instead, he threaded his fingers through hers and pinned their linked hands on either side of her head. "I'm strict about a lot of things."

With that, he angled his talented hips and unleashed a series of rough, rapid strokes that sent her flying, and all she could do was call his name.

Firm lips covered hers and devoured every ragged cry. Abruptly, the rhythm changed. Deep thrusts and shallow withdrawals subjected her to a whole new barrage of pleasure. His big frame froze, shuddered, and then their kiss reversed. His groan flowed into her mouth at the same moment his release flowed into her body.

Several minutes ticked by while her heart rate subsided. At least she thought it was hers. Two hundred pounds of rock-solid male lay over her, and the steady drumbeat hammering her ribs might just as easily belong to him. A deep, satisfied sigh rumbled up from between them. Probably his.

She closed her eyes, concentrated on the contentment of the moment. Clung to it.

When he kissed a ticklish spot near her ear, she smiled and wiggled her fingers in their still-twined hands. "Thank you for taking care of me."

"My pleasure." He rolled off her and tucked her against him. "But I think we both know you're the one taking care of me."

Chapter Seventeen

Beau steered the Yukon into the semicircle of his parents' driveway and stopped in the extra space alongside the garage of the redbrick colonial with black shutters and dark shingle roof. Massive twin maples dominated the front yard. A wreath with a big red bow graced the front door, and a Christmas tree winked from the large window of the front room. Aside from the seasonal touches, everything seemed about the same as the last time he'd been there—back in mid-October when he'd spent a weekend helping them unpack.

His parents had emailed pictures of the now-finished basement, so he knew looks could be deceiving. A part of him identified with the house a little. Chances were he looked the same on the outside, too, but inside, he'd undergone changes. Last time he'd visited he'd been alone, and content to stay that way. Well, "content" overstated things. More like stable. Comfortably numb. This time his emotions were anything but stable or comfortable. The reason for the change sat beside him, snoozing in the passenger seat.

The arrangement they'd entered into had seemed

so straightforward. Ridiculously convenient. Dumb luck had taken care of the setup, and a well-timed opportunity provided a natural end. Except the end didn't feel so natural anymore. In fact, the end felt like the most artificial part of the entire plan. Since the night of his holiday party when she'd mentioned the possibility of signing with the Mercer Gallery and withdrawing from the fellowship, he'd practically had to swallow his tongue to keep from uttering the most selfish and terrifying four-letter word in his vocabulary.

Stay.

Out of the question. *Want* he could handle. Not comfortably, no, because he didn't want to want anybody or anything, but he'd lost the battle with want before they'd exchanged more than neighborly smiles. A guy didn't ask a woman to stay because he wanted her. *Stay* implied *need.*

He sure as hell didn't want to need her, and he flat-out refused to fall in love with her, but every time he thought about her, some defective brain cell in the back of his mind whispered the damn word. *Stay.* He turned to her now and got a jolt of surprise to find her staring back at him.

"You look like Bruce Banner right before he turns into the Hulk."

"I do not."

She clenched her teeth, furrowed her brow, and made a growling sound.

"I'm fine." But he deliberately relaxed his jaw. "How are you feeling?" Late nights at the studio were starting to take a toll on her. She'd woken this morning with an upset stomach and a noticeable lack of energy, and then promptly fallen asleep once they'd gotten under way.

"Good. I think I slept off whatever nasty old bug was trying to sink its teeth into me." She sat up and stretched indulgently, folding her arms above her head and arching her body so only her hips and the back of her head touched the seat.

Hell, he felt good just watching her. She caught him looking, and the corner of her mouth lifted. "If we do what you're thinking, right here in the front of your truck while parked in your parents' driveway, Santa's going to put us on the naughty list for life."

Little did she know, his parents had gone to Chattanooga for a Christmas party. "They won't be home for hours, so we can take this inside."

"That's a relief."

"Don't be too relieved." He got out, intending to round the Yukon and help her down, but she met him at the rear of the vehicle, already holding their garment bag containing his suit and her dress for tomorrow night's Christmas Eve dinner. "If we do everything I have in mind, you're still going to end up on the naughty list."

"The naughty list is more fun anyway."

He lowered her rolling carry-on bag to the pavement and extended the handle, and then hefted his weekend bag onto his shoulder. "Okay then. Prepare to have a lot of fun." With the warning hanging in the air, he walked toward the house.

Inside, they found a note from his mom listing everything edible in the house—because she always assumed he'd arrive home blind and starving—and promising a surprise downstairs. That worried him. The whole downstairs had been remodeled. Wasn't that surprise enough?

"Oh, wow. This is nice," Savannah said as they descended the basement stairs. He had to agree. The space he associated with linoleum floors and manufactured "wood" paneling now welcomed them with dark hardwood floors, a white slipcovered sectional positioned across from a flat screen, and smooth walls decorated with framed black-and-white photographs of local landmarks.

Savannah toed her shoes off and approached one of the

pictures. "Who's the photographer?"

"Dad."

"He's got a good eye."

"I'll tell him you said so." He hauled their bags through a freshly painted six-paneled door and found the guest room, complete with a king-size bed, and an adjacent bath.

While he deposited their luggage next to a light blue upholstered wing chair, Savannah hung their garment bag in the small closet and then flopped backward onto the bed. The overstuffed down comforter accepted her weight with an airy puff and bounced the large, fabric-covered book someone had placed against the pillows. "They've turned their basement into heaven."

"My version of heaven has full-height ceilings, and no risk of me knocking myself out on a doorway header."

She moved the book to her lap and hurled a pillow at him. "Ceiling height wouldn't be an issue if you were horizontal."

He caught the pillow and tossed it back on the bed. The mattress squeaked as he braced himself over her on one hand and one knee. He would have lowered himself until he pinned her hips with his, but he noticed the book on her lap. "What is that?"

"I don't know. It was on the bed." Her lips tipped up in the off-center smile that always got him hard. "Maybe your parents left you a how-to manual?"

He dropped down beside her and flipped the book over. Someone—presumably his mom—had taped a small envelope to the front, with Savannah's name inked across the white paper. "Yeah. That's why your name is on it."

"I love surprises." She sat up and pulled the envelope off the book. A second later she unfolded a note card and read aloud. "'Welcome to the family, Savannah. Love, Cheryl & Trent.' Oh." Her smile wavered. "They shouldn't have."

"Damn right they shouldn't have." She was still focused

on the card, but he could see the front of the book now that the envelope was gone. Not a book at all—a photo album. And the photo positioned front and center on the cover? A fat, bald, bare-assed baby.

"Oh my God, is that you?"

He swiped the book from her lap. "No."

The mattress squeaked again as she scrambled to her knees and faced him. "It *is* you." She made a grab for the album. "And that's mine."

He held it out of her reach. "Possession is nine-tenths of the law."

She very slowly, very deliberately slid her hand between his legs, cupped his balls through his jeans, and gave a menacing squeeze. "Drop the book or kiss 'em goodbye."

A man had his pride, and then he had his *pride*. He held out the book.

She nabbed it from his outstretched arm like a greedy child offered a favorite treat, and then rolled over on her stomach, propped the album against the headboard, and wiggled her hips to get comfy. "Look at you." She gazed at the picture. "Same eyes. Same chin. Same adorable butt."

He stretched out beside her and set about distracting her by nuzzling the side of her neck. "You know, if you're hankering for gratuitous nudity, I'm right here. You don't have to settle for a bunch of old pictures."

She tipped her head to give him better access and flipped the book open. "I'm pretty sure I can have both."

Damn. Time to up his game. He sneaked a hand under her skirt and stroked the smooth skin of her inner thigh. "How 'bout you close the book and focus on—"

"Oooh." She tapped the page. "If I find a fuzzy red hat, maybe you'll reenact this pose for me later?"

He glanced down at the album to see a picture of him propped up in front of the Christmas tree, naked—again—

save for the Santa hat perched on his head. He sincerely hoped they hadn't used the shot for their holiday card that year. Or this year. Or ever.

"Jesus, this really is gratuitous. You'd think I didn't own any clothes for the first year of my life." He ran the edge of his teeth along her neck and eased her skirt up a few inches.

"I think, technically, the hat counts as an item of clothing." The smart-ass comment came out slightly breathless as his hand roamed higher on her thigh. She flipped the page and revealed a shot of two ridiculously chubby babies in a bathtub—one girl, one boy. The boy leaned forward to plant an openmouthed kiss on the girl, and the camera caught her midwail. "Our first kiss."

He peered at the picture more closely. Things just got interesting. "Is that you?"

"Yep."

"Hard to believe we were ever the same size." He palmed the back of her thigh and shifted her legs apart.

She turned her head and looked down her nose at him, but the little shiver she couldn't suppress undermined the imperious expression. "I'll have you know as a baby I was in the ninetieth percentile for length and weight. One of us happened to…normalize…over time."

Since it was there, and presented such a tempting handful, he squeezed her butt. "You're the normal one?"

"Perfectly." She squirmed in his grasp.

"Trust me, Smith, there's nothing normal about you."

"Montgomery, you can kiss my ass."

"Can I?" He hitched her skirt up to her waist, revealing the ass in question. "I like these." He traced one edge of her little purple panties.

She sucked in a breath and craned her neck around to glare at him. "Are you trying to distract me?"

"I'm just following orders, ma'am." He let his breath

feather over one half-bare curve, and watched goose bumps appear on her skin. "Don't mind me. Go on and look at your pictures."

"Beau."

He kissed the exposed portion of her cheek.

"Beau…"

He kissed the other.

"Bea…oh!" Her voice rose at least an octave when he kissed her next. Then he slid his tongue up the center of her panties. She squirmed so much he had to hold her hips with both hands just to retrace the route.

"Oh God. Not again."

Hell yes. Again. Her loud, throaty cry was like a velvet glove stroking his balls, his shaft. He ached, but the simple thrill of toying with her, listening to her raw, uncensored reactions, compelled him to stay the course a little longer, go a little further.

"Not there. Don't you dare…um…oh sweet mercy… okaaaay."

For the next several minutes he coaxed a low, breathless, insanely cock-torturing serenade of pleas and threats out of her. When her words came in short, shallow pants of "No more…I can't…No more," and her panties were nothing but a wet, transparent second skin, he figured he'd gone as far as he could without risking her twisting around and kicking him in the groin. He worked an arm under her waist and flipped her around. The sudden move startled a strangely satisfying squeak out of her. While she caught her breath, he dragged her panties down, hitched her legs over his shoulders, and gripped her hips. "Where *would* you like my tongue?"

She wasted no time showing him. Heels dug into his back. Fingers tangled in his hair, twisting tighter every time he lashed her eager little clit.

Her scent filled his nose. Her taste coated his tongue.

Frantic cries reached his ears. Nothing else existed. His senses disregarded everything except her.

And then she tensed—hips raised—and let out a long, heartfelt moan.

He had her skirt off and her sweater over her head before she stopped trembling. Her fingers scrambled over the buttons of his shirt, undoing as many as she could before he tugged her bra down her arms. Her hands leaped back to his shoulders as soon as her arms were free. He filled his hands with her breasts, teasing his thumbs across the tight pink tips, loving the way she leaned in and sought his touch.

By now he knew what she liked. He cupped their warm weight, lifted and squeezed, then froze when she stiffened and drew in a sharp breath.

Immediately, he relaxed his hold. "Too rough?"

"Sorry. I guess I'm a little sensitive right now."

"I'm not sure how that earns me an apology. Seems like I'm the one with some making up to do." He lowered his head and kissed one straining nipple. "Sorry," he said against the stiff peak.

Her hands went slack on his shoulders. "You're forgiven."

He kissed the other, and she arched her back in a blatant attempt to encourage him to take her into his mouth. He waited until her fingernails dug into his skin before giving her what she wanted.

His lips closed around her breast, and her hands turned restless, pushing his shirt off his shoulders, and then abandoning the task, half done, in favor of undoing his fly. Seconds later she had his jeans open and his cock threaded through the flap of his briefs while his balls remained trapped behind unforgiving folds of denim. The not-altogether unappealing agony inspired him to take matters into his own hands.

"Hurry," she urged when he rolled aside. He yanked his

shirt off, lifted his hips, and shoved his jeans and underwear down.

He'd barely kicked them off when she slung a leg over his hip and straddled him. His hands automatically settled on her hips to steady her, and his vision went blurry because she leaned forward and shifted her hips until…a groan rumbled over his tight, dry throat as she took him in.

"Jesus, Smith. Are you trying to finish me?"

"Not yet." Then she looked down at him, smiled slowly, and started to move. Up, down, forward, back, unapologetically grinding her clit against him every time she moved. The quick strokes drove him insane.

"Savannah, you can toy with me like this for approximately five more seconds. Then I'm going to roll you under me and get this done right."

Her smile only widened, and the glint in her eye turned downright wicked. "Do that, and you miss the chance to watch me do…this." She skimmed her hands up her thighs, over her stomach, and very, very slowly closed in on her gently swaying breasts. She paused just short of touching them and raised her brows at him.

"Do it."

"Where are your manners, Montgomery?"

"Please." The word sounded more like a demand than a request, but apparently she wasn't inclined to be too exacting about tone. Those devious hands swept up to her breasts, palming them, stroking them, fondling the soft, opulent flesh. She purred deep in her throat as she caressed herself.

He was going to explode, and she damn well knew it. Eyes locked on him, she slid one hand up her throat, over her chin, and slipped her index finger into her mouth. She sucked hard enough to hollow her cheeks and he groaned out loud at the memory of that same luscious mouth sucking on him. With her finger good and wet, she withdrew it and rubbed some of the moisture against her thumb, and then gave him what he knew to be a deliberately wide-eyed look. It still worked.

"I love the way my nipples feel when they're hard, but my breasts are so sensitive today, I think a little lubrication is in order. Don't you?"

"It couldn't hurt," he managed. But it could. It could hurt him. Bad.

Her face tipped up toward the ceiling and her hair streamed down her back as she teased her nipple with her wet fingers. "Oooh. That feels good." She practically hummed the words.

Warning heat started low in his belly.

"How long do you plan to keep torturing me?" The last words came out more like a growl than actual language. The tendrils of heat wrapped around his spine, his balls.

"Oh…I don't know. At least as long as I spent facedown on the mattress while you had your way with me."

Yeah, that's what he figured. The hot tendrils wound tighter. "Too long."

"Excuse—"

He cut her off by slipping his thumb between her parted lips, because hey, he believed in lubrication, too. After her initial moment of surprise, she swept her tongue over this thumb. He inserted his index finger as well, and let her do the honors. Then he slid them out so quickly her lips made an audible *pop*, and sneaked his wet fingers between her legs. Another second and he had her clit trapped between his fingers. He squeezed. Her hand curled around his wrist. "Wait—"

But he was out of time, and so was she. The first fluttering waves of her orgasm rippled along his shaft an instant before everything inside him pulled tight. The next thing he knew, he had Savannah under him, her knees bent back to her shoulders, ankles clasped around his neck, calling his name every time he surged into her.

Jesus, he couldn't get enough of her.

You'll never get enough of her.

The fatalistic thought circled his brain for a second, but then everything faded except the sensations storming his system with near brutal intensity. They battered him, conquered him, wrung him dry until he collapsed into a shuddering, incoherent heap.

Over the rush of his own pulse in his ears he heard a voice say, "Stay."

Shit. Had he said that out loud?

The way she stilled in his arms suggested yes. And worse, a reckless part of him wasn't even sorry.

Her fingers resumed sifting through his hair. "Stay, like, in the bed, or in Atlanta?"

"The bed, definitely, but…" *You opened this door. Man up and walk through.* "Let's say Atlanta for the sake of argument."

"How would that work?" He heard no demand in her voice, just caution.

"Like it does now. But if you're determined to pack your stuff, we could see if there are any larger units available in Camden Gardens." Fuck it. *Move in with me* sounded weak. Glaringly short of *Be my everything*, and deafeningly silent about little things like marriage and children. Things she wanted. Things she deserved. Things he didn't have in him anymore. He closed his eyes and lowered his forehead to hers. "Sorry. This is coming out wrong. I don't mean to be glib. I care about you."

You care *about her? Do you mean to be an asshole?*

Incredibly, instead of slapping his face, she blinked fast, as if fighting tears. "It's the most unexpected offer I've received all week."

"Yeah, well"—he started to roll off her—"it needed to

be said."

She tightened her hold on him. "This needs to be said, too." Soft lips quivered into a fragile ghost of his favorite smile. "I love you."

Those three little words should have scared the shit out of him, but they didn't. The only scary part was the strength of his urge to say them back to her, but those self-protective instincts he'd paid too dear a price to learn tamped it down with a ruthless warning.

Don't.

Loving her put him on a slippery slope right back into the rabbit hole, and he refused to risk a second visit. Even knowing this, a greedy impulse filled him, to accept what she offered no matter how unfair of him so long as it convinced her to stick around. Some vestige of conscience forced him to be up-front.

"Savannah, I-I'm honored."

Any hint of a smile disappeared from her face.

Honored? She's not the Nobel Prize nominating committee, for Christ's sake. Don't tell her you're honored.

"Delete that. What I should have said is—hell—you have to know I feel more for you than I planned to feel for anyone, ever again, but I have limits. They exist. I can't pretend they don't, and I can't change them. Not even for you. I can't give you pledges and a bunch of promises about a future I know damn well I don't control. I'm not that guy."

Can't. Can't. Can't. That's all she's hearing. All you're giving her. What can *you do?*

"I don't make promises I'm not one hundred percent sure I can keep. That said, I promise you this: if you take me on, I'm yours—all there is of me—for as long as you'll have me."

Okay. There. That's something.

"I'm not asking for promises. I didn't tell you I loved you to challenge your limits, or coerce something out of you

you're not prepared to give." Her soft lips brushed over his, calming him, dammit, when he ought to be throwing himself at her feet. "Consider it a gift."

"Best gift I've received all week," he assured her, striving to lighten the mood. The corner of her mouth lifted. Then, before he could censor his inner asshole, he added, "Does that mean you'll stay?"

Her smile wobbled. "I think we both ambushed each other just now, Beau. Why don't we give ourselves some time to recover, and see how we feel once we're not camped out in your parents' basement?"

"I know how I feel, Savannah. I know what I want."

"Well, you're a step ahead of me, Beauregard. I know how I feel, but I don't know what I want."

Chapter Eighteen

"So we agreed to hold off on any decisions until after this visit. As if a few more days will suddenly give me clarity," Savannah added under her breath. She dumped another scoop of red, white, and green candies into a cut-glass bowl serving as a centerpiece. Was this the third or fourth scoop? She couldn't remember.

"Could 'I care about you, let's live together' be enough for you?" Sinclair added a toss of holiday glitter over the tablecloth, and they moved on to the next table. The Daughters of Magnolia Grove Christmas Eve Dinner Decoration Committee expected a certain level of productivity from its volunteers, and the stink-eye the committee chairwoman sent them suggested they needed to pick up the pace.

When the chairwoman's gaze wandered to the ladies draping boughs of greenery along the tops of the large windows gracing the banquet room at the historic Oglethorpe Inn, Savannah dropped her scoop into her candy bag and plopped down in a chair. Her stomach had been trying to turn itself inside out all morning, her energy level hovered around zero, and Sinclair had asked her the question she'd been asking herself nonstop since yesterday afternoon. She still didn't have an answer.

"I don't know. All I know right now is, fate's got a sick sense of humor. I wanted to find Mr. Right so badly I talked myself into believing that Mitch's easy I-love-yous meant something. But when I finally stumble into the real thing, I fall for a man who's afraid to love. He's convinced he's got limits, and frankly, he *wants* limits. 'I care for you, let's live together' may be as far out on the emotional limb as he's ever willing to go."

"Beau may not be able to say the words, but he makes you happy. And you make him happy. I see it, and I'm looking with very clear eyes. Since I've known you all my life, I know you wouldn't be happy in an emotionally vacant relationship."

"It's true. Despite all the walls he's erected, he's not emotionally vacant. He cares all over the place—about his parents, his coworkers…a hurt little boy in a restaurant."

"And you. Not just because he said so. A guy doesn't rush to the bathroom to hold your hair back when you're puking unless he's in deep."

"Yeah." She ran her hands through her hair, tugging hard on her scalp. "He cares about me."

"Some people don't put a lot of stock in words. They're cautious about emotions. Life's taught them to protect themselves. It doesn't mean they don't have feelings, even if they fight embracing them. Spending your time with a smart, sexy-as-sin, fundamentally decent man who cares for you sounds pretty ideal." She popped a candy in her mouth. "Who needs all the trappings?"

Trappings. Interesting term. "Trappings like marriage? Kids?"

Sinclair shrugged. "You could slip those in the 'never say never' file for now, right? People change. Wants evolve. You both might feel different in six months or a year."

And that, she realized, was exactly what she'd hoped to hear. What she wanted to believe. But it felt wrong. Mostly because she knew exactly how she'd feel in six months or a year. She knew her heart. "Wouldn't that be like accepting what he's offering under false pretenses? He's not making any promises about the future."

"What false pretense? Beau doesn't own a crystal ball. He can't say for certain what changes the future will bring, or how he'll feel later. Neither can you, for that matter. If you were older, the situation would be different, but you've got years before Father Time takes certain trappings off your table. I don't see it as false pretenses to approach this with the mind-set that you're both taking time to figure out if 'I care about you, let's live together' is enough. I know you're a sucker for a sweeping romantic gesture, but given your circumstances, his request is logical and responsible."

"What do you mean *my* circumstances?" Was her sister implying that because she'd misread a relationship in the past, her judgment sucked?

Sinclair took the chair next to her and leaned in. "Because despite your so-called engagement, you two haven't actually known each other very long. Yeah, you knew each other as kids, but that doesn't count. Basically you both got thrust into a situation of instant intimacy. Then the whole thing ignited, and now you need to figure out how deep the feelings go. He's asked you to stay and move in with him. Pretty major gesture, if you ask me, out of a man you've been...I'll call it seeing... for barely a month."

Well, when you put it like that... A complicated mess of uncertainty and confusion lifted from her shoulders. She felt a smile tug at the corner of her mouth. "So what you're saying is, I should slow down, enjoy the trip, and worry less about the ultimate destination?"

Her sister grinned and popped another candy in her mouth. "What's your hurry? It's not like you're pregnant or something."

"Right." She laughed. "It's not like I'm—" Nauseous, tired, sensitive…

Late.

Holy shit.

"Sinclair, I need a ride to the drugstore."

Savannah held the plastic wand in one shaking hand, closed her eyes, and let out a long, slow breath. *Don't panic. Give it a moment and then look again. Just open your eyes and…*

The twin pink lines stared back at her, bold and unmistakable. The darn thing might as well have been a blinking neon sign. You. Are. Pregnant.

Her phone vibrated on the bathroom counter, and an incoming text from Sinclair appeared on the screen. *+ or – ???*

She reached over and turned off her phone, then rested her forehead against the cool, hard mirror. How? Denial screamed in her mind. She hadn't missed a pill.

A soft knock at the locked bathroom door had her straightening.

"Everything okay?"

Beau's voice sent the building wave of panic crashing over her. The test slipped from her numb fingers and clattered onto the granite countertop. She quickly turned off the sink taps, which she'd turned on full blast before reading the test, in some paranoid fit. "Fine!" she called, and winced at the volume of her reply. "I'll be out in a second."

Moving in fast-forward, she dropped the wand into the small wastebasket under the sink where she'd already discarded the crumpled box it came in, and tossed a few concealing wads of tissue on top. Then she washed her hands, smoothed her hair, and waited for her pulse to stop hammering. Of their own accord, her hands dropped to the narrow waist of her red off-the-shoulder pencil dress that channeled 1950s glamour bunny in every figure-hugging inch.

A baby. A fragile combination of Beau and her sat nestled in her womb like a seed, deserving of a chance to grow and thrive. Some higher power than progestin minipills had handed them a miracle, and sneaking into the bathroom to take a test, treating the results like a dirty secret to be hidden in the depths of the wastebasket, suddenly struck her as shameful. Questions like *how* no longer mattered. The answers had no impact on the present reality. Her palms flattened protectively against her belly, and her panic subsided a little as determination took root. Ready or not, this tiny life existed. It needed care, and joy, and love. It needed *them*. And she wouldn't let it down.

She stared at her reflection for a minute and accepted another reality. Dropping a life-changer like this on Beau minutes before they were expected at a holiday party wasn't fair. She needed to pick the moment for this disclosure carefully, when they had time and privacy. A cold, clammy fist squeezed her stomach when she thought about the discussion. The best course of action would be to wait until after Christmas, confirm the pregnancy with her physician, and then have the conversation with Beau.

The fist loosened. She let out a breath and opened the door.

Beau stood in front of a mirrored closet door, knotting his tie, but his gaze roamed over her when she stepped into his line of sight. He gave up on the tie, turned, and faced her. His inscrutable expression put a wobble in her knees. Was he already regretting asking her to stay?

"How do I look?"

"Late."

Shock caused her steps to falter, and the heel of her black pump snagged in the Berber rug. Two strong arms and a rock-solid chest kept her from face-planting. "W-what do you mean, I look late?"

He stroked a hand down the hair she'd tamed into long, smooth waves to complement the dress. Clear brown eyes homed in on her mouth. "You look like you're going to be about ten minutes late to the party." Then he lowered his head and kissed every bit of gloss off her lips. "Make it fifteen," he corrected when he raised his head.

Relief fizzled through her, along with a hard, fast bolt of lust, but she slapped a hand to the center of his chest until he stopped closing in, and then she got to work on his tie. "Your parents are upstairs, no doubt ready to go. What are the chances they'll wait patiently for ten to fifteen minutes?"

His hold on her loosened. "Good point. Pencil me in for later."

She adjusted the knot in his tie to the right position, and then wiped the hints of her Scarlet Santa Gloss from his lips. He used the opportunity to take a quick, hard bite from the pad of her thumb. The move surprised a laugh out of her, along with another ridiculously powerful surge of need.

"Ow." She rubbed the red skin. "That's going to leave a mark."

"Gives you something to think about, doesn't it?"

She had plenty to think about, and spent the short drive to the Oglethorpe Inn sitting next to Cheryl in the back seat of the Yukon, only half listening to her discuss the plan for a shared Christmas Day celebration between the Smith and Montgomery families.

When they arrived, Beau ushered her into the Oglethorpe, and she wondered if tonight represented the unwitting start of a family tradition. Would their little one grow up with fond memories of holidays spent in Magnolia Grove, surrounded by the grandparents, Aunt Sinclair…Mommy and Daddy?

Her mom found them just outside the banquet room and swept her into a quick hug. "There you are. I like that dress, though not quite as much as the last one I saw you in."

She shot a glance at Beau. To her, the dress was still a sore point.

"Can't wait to see it," he said, and loosened his tie with a restless tug. "Is that Bill at the bar?"

Her mom turned and squinted at the bar set up across the room. "Yes. I took one for the team and asked him to fetch me a glass of wine after Mrs. Pinkerton corned us to get the latest gossip on the wedding." She rolled her eyes and shook her head.

"White wine?" Beau asked.

Without thinking, she pressed a hand to her stomach. "Nothing for me."

He frowned and skimmed his fingertips down her cheek. "Still not feeling well?"

His show of concern warmed her heart, but then again, the man was a paramedic. "I'm fine. I just don't want to tempt fate."

The frown didn't entirely disappear, but he nodded. "Okay. I'll be right back."

Savannah watched him thread his way through the clusters of people and tables and wondered when she'd become such a resourceful liar. A month ago, the only secret she'd harbored was Mitch's name. Now she carried the weight of too many secrets, born of one massive lie. She wasn't engaged. She had no need for a $3,000 wedding dress, and she didn't feel fine.

"Sinclair wants to speak to you." Her mother's voice intruded on her guilty thoughts.

Yeah. I'll bet she does. "Where is she?"

Two perfectly groomed blonde brows drew together

as her mom scanned the crowd. "Try the cloakroom. She headed over there a few minutes ago. I'm guessing she ran into someone she knows. Otherwise, I can't fathom what takes so long about hanging three coats. Oh, there's Doreen Hightower. Doooreeen…"

Savannah edged away and then headed in the direction of the coat closet—a rack-lined room situated between the men's and ladies' lounges. As she stepped through the door, Sinclair appeared, snagged Savannah's wrist, and tugged her into the ladies' room.

"I've been texting you for hours. What the actual fuck, Savannah?"

"Why were you lurking in the coat closet?"

Sinclair strode to the farthest end of the counter and tossed her purse. "I ducked in there to avoid Mrs. Pinkerton. I wasn't in the mood to be pumped for information."

"She's harmless."

"I beg to differ." Sinclair pinned her with a sharp stare. "But we have more important things to discuss, don't you think?"

Savannah looked over her shoulder to make sure the lounge remained empty, then turned back to Sinclair. "You're going to be an aunt." There. She'd said it out loud.

For a long moment her sister just stared at her, and she feared the reaction foreshadowed a near future full of strained silences and stunned looks, but then the dimple appeared in her cheek. She pulled Savannah into her arms and in an unsteady voice, said, "Congratulations. I'm so happy for you."

Savannah closed her eyes and clung for a moment, eternally grateful for the sincerely happy reaction. Sinclair, of all people, could have called her out on every less-than-ideal aspect of the situation, every uncertainty concerning her and Beau's relationship. And given all the challenges and uncertainties, she could have validly questioned the one decision Savannah had already made. But she didn't. She smiled, and hugged, and…sniffled?

"Oh, no. Don't you dare cry, Sinclair." She pulled away and handed her sister a bunch of tissues from the box on the counter. "If you cry, I'll cry, and then—"

The flush of a toilet cut her off. The last door in the line of stalls opened, and Mrs. Pinkerton waddled out and approached the sinks. Savannah nearly groaned out loud. "Hello, Mrs. Pinkerton."

"Hello. My, don't the Smith girls look pretty tonight."

"So do you," Sinclair said.

"Nonsense," she dismissed as she washed her hands. "I aim for comfort, at my age. Not like you youngsters. Sinclair, that dress certainly catches the eye." She dried her hands. "And you, Savannah"—she stood back and took stock—"why, you're positively glowing. Don't hide out in here all night, ladies."

When she ambled out, Savannah looked at Sinclair. "Do you think she heard?"

"She hears a lot. And she repeats every word. Have you told Beau yet?"

"I planned to talk to him when we got back to Atlanta. His parents' basement is no place to tell a man he's going to be a daddy."

"I think you should assume the whispers have started as of now. Better move your timetable up if you want him to hear it from you first."

Chapter Nineteen

Beau sat between Savannah and his father at the round table in the center of the banquet room where the Daughters of Magnolia Grove, along with plenty of friends and family, had gathered to eat, drink, and be merry. Mrs. Pinkerton stood at a lectern in front of the room, giving her annual year-in-review speech spotlighting citizens who'd celebrated a milestone during the last twelve months. The crowd applauded in response to everything from newborns to ninetieth birthdays.

He knew from years ago the evening would wind down shortly afterward. Some people would head out for Midnight Mass, and some would head home to put kids to sleep and then stuff stockings, wrap last-minute gifts, and do all the stuff parents did to make sure Santa had come and gone by the time the first little eyes blinked open on Christmas morning. Still, sitting in the room among all the neighborly goodwill reminded him the Magnolia Grove Christmas Eve dinner was a nice tradition. Catching up with people had been more fun and less uncomfortable than he'd anticipated.

At least for him. Beside him, Savannah twisted her

napkin, untwisted it, smoothed it over her lap, and then began twisting it again. All the while her eyes darted around the room. She'd been on edge all night, and he was beginning to think she'd lied her pretty little lips off earlier when she'd told him she felt better. He placed a stilling hand over her restless ones, and she nearly jumped out of her chair.

He leaned close. "Are you all right?"

Those big blue eyes bounced to him, and then back to the lectern. "Yes. I'm sorry I'm so fidgety. I just…I really need to talk to you. After this, can we drop your parents at home and go for a drive or something?"

"Sure." He kept his voice casual even though his gut tightened. They'd agreed to back-burner the whole conversation about staying, but evidently she'd given the matter more thought. Her anxious look suggested he wasn't going to be thrilled with her decision. He straightened in his chair and faced front while he racked his brain for ways to change her mind.

"…and speaking of engagements," Mrs. Pinkerton rambled on, "please join me in congratulating Laurel and Bill Smith and Cheryl and Trent Montgomery on the engagement of Savannah Smith and Beau Montgomery."

His face heated as the proverbial spotlight landed on them and the room filled with more applause. Around the table their parents beamed. Sinclair looked oddly tense, which was weird because she knew the score.

"Now, I know that's not breaking news. We all saw the announcement in the *Gazette* a few weeks ago, but I'm going to go out on a limb and speculate they're opting for a short engagement."

The comment brought some whistles and laughter, but Savannah clenched her fists and whispered, "Please don't."

"Why do I hazard such a guess? Well, let's say I got a little scoop tonight. Please join me in being the first to congratulate the happy couple on the impending arrival of Baby Smith-Montgomery!"

What? Reenergized applause drowned out the echo of the words in his ears, but everything else shifted into a disorienting slow motion. People smiled broadly. His father clapped him on the back. Savannah's mom flung her arms around her daughter. Sinclair covered her face with her hand, and Savannah…

Savannah looked up at him—he belatedly realized he'd gotten to his feet—her lips and cheeks feverish red against her ghostly skin.

"What?" he repeated, and the word came out that time. "Is it true?"

But he knew. Before her hand came to rest on her flat abdomen, before she nodded, he knew. A jumble of fragmented details suddenly clicked into a complete and undeniable picture. Nausea, low energy, her suddenly sensitive breasts. A raw and livid panic tore through him, along with a crushing sense of betrayal. How long had she known?

She stood and reached for him. "Beau, I—"

"What were you thinking?" He stepped back, away from her touch.

Now she straightened, and her mouth firmed. "I didn't plan this."

"Right. You didn't plan to buy a wedding dress either, but surprise. You've got one. How long have you known?"

"I took the test before we left for the inn."

"Then why am I finding out from Claudia fucking Pinkerton?" He raked his hands through his hair and tugged on the too-long strands. "I can't believe you would try to manipulate me like this."

"Beauregard Montgomery!" His father's voice barely registered. Hands landed on his shoulders, but he shook them off.

"Manipulate you? Like this?" Savannah flung her arms out and then let them drop to her sides. "Are you serious? Yeah, Montgomery, you fell into my trap. I lured you over to my apartment, bashed you in the head hard enough to plant this genius engagement-of-convenience scheme in your mind, and then got pregnant so, boom, you'd be stuck following through." She punched him in the chest with a closed fist. "Because of all the men in Atlanta, I set my diabolical sights on the emotionally unavailable paramedic who can barely gather up the courage to admit he 'cares' for me. I thought, 'Hell, yes, *that's* the man I want to be the father of my child—'"

"What do you mean, engagement-of-convenience?" Laurel's voice broke in.

"Mom, not now." Sinclair stepped between them. "Time-out. You"—she pointed to Beau—"you need to back off. Right now."

Somebody tried to pull him away from the table, but the temper he usually kept on a leash jerked hard in the opposite direction, even though every other instinct urged him to close his mouth and walk away—keep walking until he had himself under control or his legs broke, whichever came first.

Temper won the tug-of-war, but by the time he stood toe-to-toe with Savannah, the temper had solidified into bleak defeat that sat on his chest like a corpse. "I told you I couldn't." His voice creaked. "I told you I don't have it in me, and I told you why. It's a permanent condition, Savannah. Blind people can't see. Deaf people can't hear, and I can't…" The pressure on his chest threatened to crush him. "I can't. I have obligations, and I'll meet them, but I cannot go down this rabbit hole. Not even for you."

She shoved him, hard enough to back him up a step. "I am nobody's obligation." Another shove, but this time he held his ground. "This baby is nothing but a blessing, and if you can't see that"—she came at him one more time—"stay the hell away from us."

She wanted him gone? Fine. Gone was where he should have been weeks ago.

He remembered nothing about crossing the banquet room except people stepping out of his way, but somehow he arrived at the door. He paused there and turned back. Savannah stood in the middle of the room, a small oasis of red with her arm wrapped protectively across her stomach and unspeakable sadness in her eyes. He pushed through the doors and welcomed the sting of cold night air.

His phone started vibrating before he even climbed into the Yukon. He ignored it and put the truck in drive, following the one imperative screaming through his mind.

Escape.

Scenery zipped by as he drove along Broad Street—past the turn to his parents' house—all the way to the on-ramp and straight out of town.

When the hum of his phone became incessant, he turned it off. Savannah wouldn't call. He'd officially moved himself to the ex list, like good old One-for-Three, and she'd demonstrated clearly enough that once she was done with somebody, she was done.

They never should have gotten started.

He didn't need to hear his dad tell him he was a disgrace or listen to his mom go on about how he'd broken everyone's hearts to know he'd fucked up. He had all of that coming, and more, but right now he had to get the hell away or he was going to explode.

He spent the next two hours realizing escape wasn't as simple as getting in a vehicle and hauling ass. In the course of the last month Savannah had infiltrated every area of his life, including his car. Each time he breathed, he inhaled faint traces of her perfume. A trio of ponytail holders sat stacked on the gearshift knob. A nail file peeked out from the passenger door pocket. Some change rattled in the center console cupholder, crowned by a yellow tube of lip balm with a bee on the side. The clear concoction inside had touched her lips a hundred times...something he'd never do again. A sense of loss he didn't want, and wasn't entitled to, swamped him.

By the time he trudged up the stairs to his apartment, he craved only one thing—complete and total oblivion. A shadow by his door moved. His adrenaline surged and then subsided as a figure pushed off the wall and the light from the overhead fixture landed on Hunter.

The blond man checked his watch and then looked at Beau and raised a brown paper bag clearly containing a bottle of liquor. "Merry fucking Christmas."

"Merry fucking Christmas to you. What are you doing here?" He motioned Hunter aside and unlocked his door.

"I'm Santa's little helper. I got a call informing me your Christmas Eve didn't go as planned, and asking me to do a welfare check." Hunter followed him inside and went directly to the kitchen to get two glasses from the cabinet.

"My mom called you?"

"No. Not your mom."

Hunt poured two double shots of whiskey, and Beau flashed back to the afternoon he'd gone shot-for-shot with Savannah. And lost. Or won, depending on how one looked at it.

"My dad, then."

"Not anyone in your family." He pushed one of the glasses across the counter and took the other for himself.

"How is she?" *How do you think she is, moron?*

Hunter shrugged. "She sounded okay, I guess, given the circumstances."

Circumstances like being publicly accused of manipulation and deceit by a man she thought she loved after telling him she was pregnant with his child? He already regretted the words.

Savannah lived life openly and spontaneously. Manipulation wasn't part of her makeup. Good or bad, she held nothing back. He couldn't say the same for himself. "She told you what happened?"

"I got the gist. I didn't actually talk to her very long. I mostly spoke to someone named Sinclair, and if you're inclined to keep your balls, I'd avoid her for the next little while if I were you." He downed his drink and then gave a long, eighty-proof exhale.

Beau did the same and slid his empty glass back to Hunter.

His partner gave him a speculative look. "You ready to talk, or do you want to shut up and drink?"

Easiest decision he'd made all night. "Shut up and drink."

• • •

"You're too calm. I'm worried you're in shock." Sinclair donned oven mitts and opened her old, battered oven. The smell of apple pie wafted out even before she reached in and extracted the steaming pastry.

Maybe she was in shock, because Savannah fought an urge to laugh at the incongruity of Sinclair standing there in her high heels and racy black dress, now accessorized with flaming skull oven mitts and a piping hot pie. She didn't give in to the impulse because of a strong fear that if she unleashed her emotions, she'd soon be sobbing uncontrollably. "I'm not in shock. I'm just—" She splayed her hands on the worn surface of Sinclair's antique pine table and searched for the right explanation. "Tonight went about as poorly as it could have, but screaming and crying won't improve anything."

"And pie will?"

"They call it comfort food for a reason."

"Yeah, well, I don't know how comforting a frozen apple pie from the gas station food mart is going to be." She placed the pie on a trivet in the middle of the table alongside two forks, took off the oven mitts, and sat down across from Savannah. "Chances are it's not going to stand up to your homemade version, but my options were limited, given it's Christmas."

"How bad can they screw up pie?"

Sinclair handed her a fork and then dug into the domed center of the flaky crust with her own. "I guess we'll find out."

Savannah dug in as well. They spent a moment blowing on the steaming forkfuls.

Sinclair inhaled. "It smells good."

"It does. Looks pretty good, too."

They took bites at the same time.

"Oh my God." Sinclair's face fell. "Worst pie ever." She took another bite, as if she couldn't believe what her taste buds were telling her. "It's a crime against pie. It's crap."

"It is," Savannah agreed around a mouthful of dry, hard apple chunks, synthetic, gloppy filling, and a crumbly sawdust crust. She swallowed and, to her horror, burst into tears. "A-and I'm the worst mom ever, because I'm feeding my baby crap."

Sinclair was at her side immediately. "You're not the worst mother ever."

"I am." Crappy gas-station pie was a ridiculous trigger, but now that the tears had started, she couldn't seem to stop them. "What if I've just ruined pie for this baby forever?" She tossed her fork down. "I don't know what the hell I'm doing. I can't do this on my own."

"You're not on your own." Her sister took her by the shoulders and looked her in the eye. "You will *never* be on your own. You've got me. Mom and Dad, Beau's parents—"

"M-mom and Dad are so horrified they can't even look at m-me."

"They're in shock—angry and disappointed you lied to

them—but they'll forgive you. They love you, and they're going to love their grandchild. As for Beau's parents, let Beau deal with them...at whatever point he pulls his chickenshit head out of his ass."

"What if he doesn't?"

"He will."

"Were you not just cursing him out thoroughly to his partner on the phone an hour ago?"

"Yep. And I'll curse him out to his face, next chance I get. But I also know he cares about you. He told you so himself."

"The situation has changed. That's not good enough anymore. This baby needs a father who loves it freely and unconditionally. Not some emotionally resistant man who meets his legal obligations but refuses to get too close."

"Give him a little bit of time to get his head straight. Your getting pregnant is his worst nightmare come to life. What if something happens? What if history repeats itself? All he's focused on right now are the risks. He can't see past them, so he's trying to close himself off. The thing is, his walls were already starting to crumble. He couldn't hold out."

"He's held out pretty well for the last three years."

Sinclair folded her hands on the table and tilted her head to the side. "No. He hid out well for the last three years. He blockaded his heart and nobody got past the barriers until this Thanksgiving, when he lowered them enough to trust you with a problem and ask you for help. He let you into his life— not for the right reasons, and certainly not with the intention of falling for you—but he let you in. Now he cares for you, and I hope he loves you. He just needs to grow a pair and figure it out."

"I can't wait forever for him to figure his shit out. I have to start making plans now."

"Wait a little while, Savannah."

She folded her arms and stared at the floor. "Why should

I?"

"First, because you're in love with the man. Second, he's the father of your child, so he's always going to need a way back. Don't go to Italy without talking to him."

Savannah ran her hand over her stomach and accepted reality. "I'm not going to Italy." The words were surprisingly easy to say.

"You're not? I thought the fellowship represented the opportunity of a lifetime."

"This baby is my opportunity of a lifetime, and I don't want to have him or her five thousand miles from home. I'd actually been thinking about declining the fellowship anyway. The Mercer Gallery offered to represent me, and I trust them. I moved to Atlanta to secure a deal with a reputable gallery that could help establish me in a regional market, and if I accept the offer from Mercer, I've fulfilled that goal."

"And you have your baby at home."

Savannah nodded. "Provided home isn't located across the hall from Beau-how-could-you-manipulate-me-this-way-Montgomery. Can I move in with you for a while?"

Sinclair reached around and gave her a hug. "Crazy Aunt Clair always has room for you."

Chapter Twenty

Beau woke up on his sofa with his cheek sweat-glued to the leather and a yellow Post-it note stuck to his forehead. He peeled it off and flipped it over. The weak gray morning light filtering into the apartment assaulted his eyes, but he forced them to focus on the note. He recognized Hunter's scrawl.

Call your mother.
P.S. I'm never drinking again.

Yeah, right. He got up, astounded when his head didn't roll right off his shoulders, and dragged his sorry ass to the medicine cabinet to swallow three painkillers with a handful of tap water. Then he brushed his teeth, splashed his face with a couple more handfuls of water, and took stock.

Red eyes, scruffy jaw, the complexion of a zombie. Not much of a way to show up on his parents' doorstep on Christmas Day, but they'd seen worse — much worse — and he owed them an in-person explanation and apology. He owed Savannah's parents the same.

And you need to talk to Savannah…

Had she come home last night? If so, she'd gotten into her apartment more quietly than she'd ever managed in the past six months. He'd been listening for any telltale footfalls on the stairs, or the rattle of a key in a lock—right up until he'd passed out. His eyes dropped to the counter, where the assortment of bottles and jars and...product...had multiplied in some seemingly organic way since the first evening she'd come over with a bag full of stuff to set the scene for his parents.

This was no longer set dressing, though. He tugged off his undershirt and walked to the bedroom to change into clean clothes. His apartment—his life—had morphed into a shared space. He shouldn't have let it happen, because before she'd come along, he'd been content with his orderly, somewhat stark apartment and his orderly, somewhat isolated life. Now the thought of her things not cluttering the counter, or her discarded robe not tossed across her pillow—the thought of *her* not being there—left a dangerous void. The kind of void that would drive him to her doorstep to offer things he couldn't afford to offer.

Even realizing this, he found himself pausing between their apartments on his way out. He ran his hand over her door.

No sound.

It didn't dawn on him until he'd reached Magnolia Grove that the next sounds he'd likely hear from her apartment would be the groans of movers, because in seven days she'd board a plane to Italy. If she was still going. Would she leave now that they had a baby on the way? If she did, would she stay away the entire nine months? Give birth thousands of miles from her home, her family...him? The prospect sent a burst of useless energy through him. His fingers tightened on the steering wheel and he had to talk himself out of the impulse to drive straight to the Smiths' and tell her not to go.

First off, he didn't know if she was there. Second, he'd come off like a crazy asshole trying to play it both ways. *Don't go, but don't look to me for reasons to stay.*

The grip of last night's flight instinct had loosened enough for him to recognize they needed to talk, but he honestly didn't trust himself with the conversation. His head was all over the fucking map, but it really didn't matter which way his thoughts turned, because he knew the landscape well enough to realize there was no safe ground.

Not even here. He parked in his parents' drive. His mom opened the door before he cleared the front steps, and the disappointment in her eyes made him feel like a seventeen-year-old caught sneaking in after curfew reeking of weed and beer. Except this was worse.

"I'm sorry."

Tired eyes searched his face. "Why?"

"For lying. For—"

"Not why are you sorry." Her eyes flashed with impatience. "Why did you lie?"

"It's a long story, Mom, and the whys don't change anything. Can't we just leave it at sorry?"

"No. I don't think we can. We've left too much at sorry these last few years, and this is where it's gotten us. You've lied. Savannah's lied on your behalf. Her parents are hurt, and angry. Under the circumstances, your father and I have plenty of time for a long story. Come inside, sit down, and start at the beginning."

Apparently he didn't have much choice. He let her pull him into the house and drop him in a chair at the end of the kitchen table. His father slid a mug of coffee in front of him, along with two aspirin, and took the chair to his left. His mother took the one on his right. He opened his mouth—to say what, he didn't know—but the whole story came spilling out. By the time he got to the part about waking up on his sofa with a staggering hangover and the note from Hunter, he was emotionally exhausted and unable to meet their eyes.

His father sat back in his chair and let out a long, slow breath. "Now that you know your mother's going to be fine, we can revert back to the natural order of things, where the parents worry about the kid. Not vice versa."

"I'm fine. You don't need to worry about me."

"Oh, yeah. You're fine," his father observed. "What about Savannah? What about the baby?"

"I'm handling it."

"How? By running away?"

"I'll answer to her for that—"

"I expect you will."

"Look, last night took me by surprise, and I'm not proud of how I reacted, but the bottom line remains. I can't deliver the happy ending, okay? I don't have it in me." But he might have a panic attack in him. His throat felt tight, and someone had parked a backhoe on his sternum.

"Beau," his mom interjected. "You're spending so much of your energy stifling your emotions you don't know what you have in you. And you're so determined to avoid getting hurt, you don't see you're doing more damage than God, or fate, or luck ever could." She took his hand and squeezed, as if she could wring something out of him. "How do you *feel* about Savannah?"

He shook his head. Speech was out of the question.

His mom rubbed his hand. "Thanksgiving Day, when you told us you and Savannah were engaged, I was really happy to hear the news, but on the drive home I admitted to your father I had concerns. I saw two people with a lot of chemistry between them, and some easy affection—I think that's one of Savannah's gifts—but no real emotional connection. I told Trent I thought you two were in lust, not love. But I had hope because chemistry and affection had gotten you to the point where you were willing to take a chance on something deeper. I staked a lot on that willingness."

"I know. I'm sorry. I'll reimburse you and Savannah's mother for the dress."

She waved the comment aside. "I'm not talking about financial stakes. Here's the thing, a week later, when we had dinner together, I saw two people in tune to each other. While I discussed my upcoming surgery, she sensed your anxiety and reached for you, and you held on to her. Took comfort from her touch. That night I said to myself, 'Aha. It's not all fun and games. He's fallen.'"

He shook his head. The weight on his chest paralyzed him. "I can't—"

"You already have. Done deal, Beau. The only question is whether you're brave enough to face up to your feelings and strong enough to convince Savannah to trust you with hers. I believe she's at Sinclair's, if you want to find out."

His heart pounded like a Code 3. His lungs couldn't seem to pull in enough air. But even in the midst of a full physical meltdown, one terrifyingly clear thought lodged in his mind. His mom was right. He hadn't meant to. God knew he hadn't wanted to, but he'd fallen in love with Savannah, and she was going to have their baby. He'd gone all-in weeks ago, whether he liked it or not.

His mom patted his hand and stood. She padded out of the kitchen and returned a minute later holding a large box in her arms. "This is for you. Merry Christmas."

He got up and took it from her. "What is it?"

"A couple good things came out of my cancer diagnosis, one being I finally organized all our boxes of photos into albums. I thought you should have these."

"More naked baby photos?" His smile felt weak.

"Among others. I hope you'll look through them when you get some time. Share them with Savannah."

He lowered his head to accept her hug and kiss.

His dad said, "Good luck," and then he was back in the Yukon, staring out the windshield at the slate of gray sky, wondering how the hell to go about begging Savannah's forgiveness for his behavior last night. How could he convince her to trust him? Beyond "I'm sorry" and "I love you," nothing sprang to mind. His mom had nailed it. He was years out of practice doing stuff like talking things out and explaining his feelings. *You're gonna have to get better at it, starting now.*

He had a vague idea of where Sinclair lived, and steered the truck along the lonely back road in the direction of the Whitehall Plantation. The antebellum stone and plank barn rose behind a screen of willow trees that managed to look like giant, graceful artifacts with their bare winter branches. He pulled into the packed dirt driveway and bounced along under the leafless canopy until the big, rolling wooden doors came into view. Then he spotted Sinclair in the yard, adding seed to a bird feeder. She dropped the scoop into the bag on the ground and dusted her hands off on her jeans as he rolled to a stop. By the time he stepped out, she'd made it to the side of the truck.

"Hi—" That's as far as he got before her palm connected with his cheek and the air around them echoed with the impact. It could have been worse, he acknowledged as the sting subsided. He'd seen a Smith girl throw a punch.

She shook out her hand. "Merry Christmas, Montgomery. You look like shit."

"Thanks. Merry Christmas to you, too. Is Savannah available?"

Her body language told him the slap wasn't all the punishment he should expect. She folded her arms and rocked back on the flat heels of her tall black boots. "As a matter of fact, she's not."

"My parents told me she's here."

"I didn't say she's not here. I said she wasn't available."

He pressed his fingers to his brow bone in an attempt to ease the tension headache blooming behind his eye socket. "I realize I'm on your shit list, and hers, and pretty much everybody's at this point, but there's more to resolve here than the fact that I acted like an asshole last night. I need to talk to her."

"I'll let her know you stopped by and give her the message."

"Goddammit, Sinclair—"

She marched up to go head-to-head with him. "Look, she's asleep, finally, and I'm not going to wake her. She's exhausted. If you want to talk to her, you're going to have to wait until she's ready to have a conversation. I don't think that's too much to ask, do you?"

Fuck. He exhaled slowly and stared hard at the horizon. "No. I don't think that's too much to ask."

"Go home, Beau." Sinclair turned and walked toward her door. "Savannah will be in touch when she's ready."

. . .

Savannah trudged up the stairs to her apartment for the first time since she and Beau had left to spend Christmas at home, like the happy couple they'd been pretending to be. Now, seven days later, the pretense was over, leaving behind a very real consequence. Officially real, as of today, though she'd never had much doubt.

Beau's door swung open before she reached the landing, and he stepped out. She'd tried her best over the last few days to prepare for seeing him again. To steel herself against the feelings.

"You're here." His dark, shadowed eyes met hers, and in their depths she saw some of the same things she saw in her own eyes these days—stress, fatigue, worry.

She shrugged. "You got my text yesterday. I told you I'd be home this evening if you wanted to talk."

"And I told you I wanted to talk. Anytime, anywhere. It's been days, Savannah. If you wanted to punish me with silence, you accomplished the goal."

She could see the truth of that in his eyes, too, and guilt hacked away at her conscience. "I wasn't trying to punish you." Not much, anyway. "I wanted to have concrete information before I spoke to you again. I felt an obligation to improve over the haphazard way information came out Christmas Eve." She reached into her purse and retrieved the lab report she'd received from her doctor earlier in the day. "Here."

He took the paper, but didn't take his eyes off her. "What is it?"

"Blood test results. It's more foolproof than the drugstore test I took Christmas Eve, but entirely consistent. I'm pregnant." With that, she turned and unlocked her door. "Would you like to come in?"

He put the report in his pocket and followed her inside. "I never doubted you," he said quietly. "How are you? Does everything look okay at this point?"

"Everything looks fine. I'm about three weeks along. I asked my doctor how I got pregnant while on the pill, and I guess with the type of pill I use, I needed to be very diligent about taking them at the same time of day—"

"You're moving," he interrupted, glancing around her packed and considerably cleared out apartment.

"Yes. Sinclair and I have been packing and moving stuff for the last few days."

"I didn't realize. I mean, I knew you'd been here Sunday, because you moved your things out of my apartment, but I've been working a 12/4."

"I know. I left your key under your mat. Did you get it?"

"Yes. Don't go."

Her heart skipped a couple beats, but she kept her voice calm. "Why not?"

"Because I love you." The words came out like a criminal's confession. He raked a hand through his hair and took a step back. "I didn't plan to fall in love with you. I wasn't looking for that to happen." He retreated another step. "But it did."

"Beau..." She took a step toward him, and he retreated again, until he had the wall at his back.

"The whole thing scares me to death. You...the baby... feeling this intensely about something again, but I can't shove the emotions into some closet and lock them away. They're there, and there's nothing I can do but accept them. And I have. I told you before Christmas I didn't make promises unless I was one hundred percent sure I could deliver. I swear to God, Savannah, if you trust me, I won't run again. I'll be there for you and this baby. I promise."

Something hot splashed on the hand she had pressed to her chest, and she realized she was crying. She scrubbed her palm over her cheeks to wipe away the tears. "I'm sorry, Beau. I know this is hard for you, and I don't want to appear ungrateful for all the soul-searching you've done, and everything you've said, but I can't move forward if this is how you feel."

"You can't stay if I love you, and promise to be here for you and the baby?" He shook his head, rejecting her refusal. "I don't understand."

"I can't stay because you don't *want* to love me. In your own words, you're terrified. You're trapped by your feelings. Look at you," she went on, gesturing toward him when he would have interrupted. "You couldn't even finish the conversation without backing yourself into a corner."

He pushed away from the wall and closed the distance between them. "My anxiety isn't a reflection on you or the baby. It's about risks I have absolutely no control over—and yes, they terrify me. I can't erase my past."

"I know. And I understand your fears. Honestly, I do. If it were just you and me, I could be patient and hope your reluctant love evolved into something more enthusiastic and generous, but it's not just you and me. Our baby deserves joyful, enthusiastic, generous love, right from the start." She hesitated as he prowled the room like a caged animal, but then added the last bit of truth. "Just like your first one."

"That's not fair. I'm not the same man I was three years ago, and there's nothing—nothing," he repeated, and pounded a fist on the wall, "I can do about it. Don't you think I wish I could be that guy again? Don't you think if I had the power to magically change, I would? Tell me how to do it, Savannah, and I will."

Her heart broke for him...and for herself. "I don't know how to help you let go of the fear. I wish I did. I can only tell you what we need. Accepting anything less is unfair to all of us." There was nothing left to say, and standing there crying wouldn't change anything. She hitched her purse straps onto her shoulder and walked to the door. "I have to go."

"Fine." He stepped in front of her, blocking the door. Tension radiated from every line of his body. "I'll figure it out. I'll go to therapy, or church, or whatever you want. Just don't leave."

"This isn't about you jumping through hoops to satisfy me. That's not the right answer. Go to therapy if *you* want to go to therapy. Attend church if you think faith will help you find what you need."

"You're the one putting me in a trap now. There's nothing I can say at this moment to convince you to stay with me."

She swallowed the lump in her throat and walked past him into the hallway. "I'll text you updates on the baby, if you'd like."

He dropped his head and stared at the ground for a long moment, and she thought he might tell her to go to hell, but when he finally looked up, his expression was impossible to read. "I'd appreciate that." A few long strides brought him into the hall beside her. "I'd appreciate hearing from you in general."

She locked the door and then went up on her tiptoes and kissed his cheek. "I can do that." It took every ounce of her willpower not to wrap her arms around him and burrow into his strength. His warmth. The weakness came out in the form of one last, long inhale, to commit his scent to memory. She pulled away before her resolve crumbled. Blinking back tears, she muttered, "Take care of yourself." And she left.

Chapter Twenty-One

Beau wandered around his living room, unable to sit still. Traps were the theme of the evening, and right now, the four blank white walls of his apartment felt like one. Since Sunday night when he'd come home from work to find Savannah's things gone, the lack of warmth and energy in the space had hit him like a fist to the gut. How had he lived like this for so long?

Only one splash of color drew his eye. The glass bouquet Savannah had made sat on his end table. The little serpent mocked him from the rim. He looked away, and his gaze snagged on the box his mom had given him for Christmas, which he'd placed on the coffee table days ago and not bothered to move. He walked over to it and lifted the lid. Four photo albums rested inside. One he recognized from his trip down memory lane with Savannah. Seeing the light blue cover brought too many recent memories bubbling to the surface. He grabbed a white album instead and sat on the couch.

A satin ribbon looped into a bow across the front of the

album, and something about that made his stomach clench. He opened the cover to reveal a protective parchment paper page with the words "Our Wedding" embossed in silver. Shit. He almost closed the album, but he could already see an image through the thin paper. He turned the page and confronted a black-and-white portrait of Kelli decked out in her wedding gown, standing in front of a large window covered by thin white drapes. Her back was to the camera, her radiant face in profile and a gentle smile curving her lips. She looked young and happy. Incredibly alive.

The next page featured a funny shot of Kelli and her bridesmaids doing a Zoolander supermodel thing for the camera. He kept flipping—his dad had been busy that day—and paused to look at a picture of his groomsmen and him dressed in their tuxes, playing Texas Hold'em in the suite before the ceremony. He'd gone all-in, and won, thanks to drawing into four-of-a-kind on the river to beat Hunter's full house. Yeah, he'd been one lucky bastard back then.

There were shots of the reception, him and Kelli feeding each other cake, Hunter giving a best-man toast Beau had yet to live down, Kelli and him in each other's arms, taking their first dance as husband and wife. The album ended with a picture of them standing in an alcove at the reception, kissing. God, he'd loved her. He remembered the moment clearly, remembered practically bursting with happiness he never once stopped to second-guess. The guy in the picture had no fear. Then again, the guy in the picture had no fucking clue what the future held.

He put the album aside and reached for the next one. The pink quilted cover warned him, but he pulled it out anyway. A tiny pink handprint filled one photo square on the front of the book, and an only slightly larger pink footprint filled the other. Beneath, dark pink letters spelled "Abbey." He ran his finger over the little palm print. So small and perfect. Acid hot tears blurred his vision, but he wiped them away with an impatient hand and opened the cover.

And there she was.

Hi, baby. Sorry Daddy's such a mess. I didn't expect to see you today.

He traced her sweet newborn face, all cheeks, squinting eyes, and pouty little mouth. The barest hint of a pointed chin just like her mother's.

Jesus. A wounded animal sound wrenched up from his chest, but he couldn't look away. He flipped the pages, greedily drinking in pictures. Kelli in the hospital bed, holding Abbey in her arms and glowing like an angel despite five hours of labor and no epidural. Him, standing by the window, grinning like an idiot and holding Abbey for the first time.

He kept turning pages. There were a surprising number of pictures considering she'd only been four months old when he'd lost her. The shot of her dressed like a pumpkin for her first Halloween pried a laugh out of him, as did a black-and-white photo of her in her baby bath, splashing herself in the face and giggling. She smiled a lot. And everyone around her smiled, too. Grandma, Mommy…Daddy. He closed the book and ran his hand over the cover. Those four months had been the happiest of his life.

The last album still sat in the box. Curious, he wiped his cheeks and lifted it out. The bright yellow cover shone like a sunbeam. He opened the book, brushed past the parchment paper, and stared at the empty page. A flip through the other pages quickly confirmed they were all empty. He turned back to the parchment page and spotted his mother's handwriting on the inside corner of the cover.

This album is for you to fill with new memories.
Love, Mom & Dad

...

"Have you talked to Savannah yet?"

Hunter's question pulled him away from his silent countdown. Tick-tock. Six p.m., New Year's Eve. By tomorrow at this time, she'd be somewhere over the Atlantic, winging her way to Venice.

"I sent a text to wish her luck tonight."

"A good luck text? Hell, if that doesn't convince her to stay, I don't know what will."

If Hunter hadn't been driving the rig tonight, he would have punched him. "I told her I loved her, and I wanted her to stay."

"You presented it wrong."

Really, Einstein? "I presented it honestly. It's not good enough for her."

"And you know what? I respect her for calling you on your weak-assed bullshit. Life's full of risk. Bad things happen to good people. Nobody knows this better than us. But good things happen, too. Savannah, for instance. She's the best thing to happen to you in a long time. Same goes for the baby. Some people would give up a kidney to fall in love and be loved in return. I have a cousin who's going through all kinds of crap right now to try to conceive. You've been given these gifts a second time. Focus on the good, and muster up some fucking optimism, instead of acting like you're in love with her against your will—"

A call crackled over the radio, interrupting the Dr. Phil show. Beau picked up and listened as the dispatcher sent them onto the freeway in response to a fender-bender involving a vague report of a female passenger in distress. Hunter turned on the lights and siren, while Beau directed him to the scene.

"Motherfuckers," Hunter cursed, honking at the slow-to-react drivers reluctant to give up their place in the bumper-to-bumper traffic. "I hope some dickhead drags his ass when you're the one waiting for help."

By the time they got to the scene a police cruiser had arrived and officers had placed flares around a late-model minivan with barely a scratch on it and an old Subaru Outback with a crunched-in rear bumper. Hunt pulled in behind the cruiser. Beau grabbed the primary response kit and headed toward the officer standing beside the minivan, talking to a middle-aged man who was presumably the driver of that vehicle. The officer waved him to the other car. Hunter fell into step beside him as he approached the Outback. He saw a female officer standing by the back passenger-side door, leaning into the car. He heard a woman cry out—the kind of cry that started low and slowly escalated to a scream—and quickened his pace. "What have we got?"

The young female officer scrambled away from the car as if there was a ticking bomb inside. "The miracle of birth. Thank God you're here. I was trying to time the contractions but they're coming so fast—"

"Where are you going? Don't leave!" The frantic voice came from the backseat.

"You're attending," Beau said, and hung back to let Hunter assess the patient.

Hunter asked for the woman's name, but the officer shook her head. "We haven't gotten that far."

And here's why his partner made the better lead on this call. Hunter simply pasted on his reassuring smile and stuck his head into the backseat. "Hey there, Ms.—"

"Where's the woman? Lady, come back. Please!"

Hunter hunkered down. "She's a state trooper. I'm a paramedic. Right now, you want me."

"I want a woman! Call another paramedic. Please. I'll wait...I'll—" Her breath hitched, and she braced against a new wave of pain. "Jeeeesuuuus. It huuuurts."

"If you let me take a look, I might be able to do something about the pain."

Beau left Hunter trying to talk her out of her panties and ran to get the panic pack. He returned in time to hear the mother-to-be say, "Oh God. I can't believe I'm going to give up my underwear to a fast-talking guy with a pretty face. These kinds of decisions are what got me into this in the first place." The sentence ended in another breathless cry.

"Would it help if I told you I'm gay?"

Beau put on gloves and then handed Hunter a pair, and admired his partner's ability to think on his feet.

"Maybe," the woman panted. "Are you?"

Hunter gloved up and offered her a grin. "Me and this guy"—Hunter nodded at him—"have been partners for a long time. Say hi, Beau."

Beau leaned his head in and waved at the very young, very pretty, very scared woman stretched out in the back seat. "Hi...?"

"Madisonnnnn... Holy shiiiit."

Hunter took the sterile drape Beau offered him and waited until the contraction passed before speaking.

"Nice to meet you, Madison. I'm Hunter. I'm going to help you lift your hips, so I can slide this little sheet under you. Then we're going to see what's going on with this baby. It is just one baby, right?"

"One," he heard her confirm as he moved aside to provide them a measure of privacy, and arranged supplies in the order Hunter would need them.

Madison's voice carried from inside the car. "Hunter, I really need something for the pain now."

"I can't, honey. You need to push."

"No...no...no." The car rocked. "I'm not due yet. I have another three weeks."

"Babies don't have calendars, Madison," Hunter replied

calmly. "I've done this more than once. Trust me, it's time to push."

Their patient had other ideas. "Do something to keep her in! It's too soon. What if she can't…?" The arrival of the next contraction interrupted the what-ifs, but not before Beau filed away another important piece of information. A girl. Madison expected a girl. Memories tried to intrude, but he forced them away and focused on the job. Studies indicated newborn girls were generally smaller and had few complications. Good news, given the circumstances.

"Three weeks is nothing, sweetheart. Counts as full-term," Hunter assured her. "Have you been seeing a doctor every now and then? Have your checkups been good?"

"Yes," she replied between pants. "I saw my doctor right after Christmas. Everything's on track." Her voice turned stubborn. "I'm due in three weeks."

The next contraction set in, contradicting her. Conversation subsided as her recovery time between contractions diminished. Hunter alternately encouraged her and bullied her through transition.

Eventually, though, her end of the dialogue devolved to gasping, defeated phrases like "I can't," and "No more." He quietly asked Hunter if he should get the gurney. They'd have to transport her if things stalled. She'd need more support than they could give her.

"Uh-uh," Hunter answered. "Not yet. My girl Madison's going to do this, right, sweetheart? You're ready to meet this baby you've been taking such good care of for the last nine months. Hold her in your arms and show her what a strong, brave, pretty mama she's got."

Madison sounded less than convinced, despite Hunter's impressive confidence. He listened with half an ear as Hunter gave her a pep talk, and mentally worked out the logistics of loading her into the rig and navigating the traffic to the nearest ER. He could get it done in ten minutes—fifteen max. With his mind so deep in plan B, he almost didn't hear his partner say, "Beau's going to come around to your side and climb in. He'll support you while you push, okay? He's way more comfortable than a hard car door."

Okay, plan B went on hold for now. He hurried to the other side of the car and got in. She more or less fell against him.

"That's right." Beau turned so his chest supported her back. "Let me take your weight." As she relaxed, he gently inched her hips closer to Hunter. His partner spared him a grateful glance.

The next contraction hit hard. When it finally let go, his partner had the head in view, but Beau had an armful of exhausted, trembling, and borderline incoherent woman. He caught Hunter's eye and nodded toward the ambulance. *Transport her.*

Hunter shook his head, and then called Madison's name in a sharp voice.

To Beau's surprise, she responded. Hunter's smile mirrored his own relief.

"Stay with me, sweetheart," Hunter said. "Next time, when the contraction comes, I want you to push as long as you can. Not hard, but long. Got it?" While Hunter issued the instructions, he placed supplies on the drape.

Madison's small frame stiffened as the next spasm gripped her. She leaned forward and put her whole body into the push. Beau supported her with one hand between her shoulders and the other against her lower back.

"Oh God. Oh God. Oh God."

In his mind he added a few *Oh God*s of his own to the mix. Apparently God was listening, because Hunter called, "That's my girl. You're doing great." The moment of triumph was short-lived, however, because he followed with an urgent instruction to stop pushing.

Beau held the whimpering woman, feeling helpless as shakes rattled through her. Hunter moved quickly, his attention locked on the action in front of him. Beau couldn't see much from his position, but he knew enough about the process to realize Hunter was dealing with a cord situation, and prayed he could resolve it. Transporting now, with mother and baby in distress due to an unmanageable nuchal cord, would be a nightmare.

He almost high-fived his partner when Hunter said, "Sweetheart, you're almost done. One last push…there you go…a little more." Next thing he knew, Hunter had a baby in his hands. Her little chest expanded; Beau released a breath of his own. While Hunter cleaned, dried, and wrapped the infant, Beau eased Madison into a more reclined position and attempted to check her pulse.

The new mom had different priorities and kept trying to sit up. "Is she all right? Is she breathing?"

As if activated by the sound of her mother's voice, the baby cried out. The little bleating sound told him she wasn't having any problem drawing in air.

Hunter grinned. "Aw. Is that any way to say thank you? Want to go to your mama?" He placed the baby into Madison's outstretched arms.

Beau took the additional towels Hunter handed him, and then the stethoscope. "Hey, Madison?" He waited until she turned her head and smiled at him.

"Isn't she beautiful?"

"She's gorgeous." And she was. Pink and vigorous. "Your first post-birth duty as a mom is to hold her and keep her warm while I listen to her heart and lungs."

Heart rate and respiration were strong and steady. He helped Madison listen to her baby's heartbeat while Hunter clamped and cut the cord. Beau collected some medical history while his partner dealt with stage three. The cops made themselves useful and got the stretcher out of the rig, and then finally, Beau held the baby while Hunter lifted Madison onto the stretcher.

He walked behind them, staring into the newborn's blurry eyes, and overheard Madison ask, "Back in the car, when you promised my baby and me would be okay, how did you know?"

Hunter looked back at Beau before answering. "Gotta have faith in happy endings. Otherwise, what's the point?"

Good question.

He pondered it for the drive to the hospital, and back to the station, and the same answer kept shoving its way to the front of his mind, along with an epiphany he needed to share with a specific someone. Now. By the time they'd clocked out he was frantic to get to Savannah.

"You headed home?" Hunter asked, apparently oblivious to his urgency.

"Not exactly, no. You?"

"I'm thinking about making a stop by the hospital, just to check in on our last call."

"Good job tonight." He clapped a hand on Hunter's shoulder. "You did everything right."

Hunter grinned. "I was sweating like a damned soul running a marathon in hell."

"It didn't show."

"I have this philosophy I cling to when shit starts flying."

"What's that?"

"Things might just work out."

Chapter Twenty-Two

Savannah stood in the crowded gallery, smiling and nodding appreciatively as a prominent art critic held court for a handful of local collectors and discussed her work. Normally she loved the energy and buzz of a showing, but tonight the bustle of people and hum of conversation made it hard for her to concentrate on anything. Instead, her attention kept drifting to the milling guests.

Stop looking for him. Why would he come?

And yet she couldn't prevent her eyes from searching the crowd. Midnight loomed, but the showcase remained in full swing. She'd sold several pieces, which meant she ought to be ecstatic. At least one aspect of her life was finally going according to plan.

The critic said something that coaxed a laugh out of the group of people around her. Savannah managed a lackluster chuckle that got lost in the noise of the room. A man in a suit entered the gallery, and her gaze snagged on him. A flare of recognition subsided into disappointment as their eyes locked. His lit up and familiar lips curved into a fast smile.

Mitch. Not the man from her past she'd been hoping to see tonight. Apparently her disappointment didn't show, because he made his way over. She excused herself from the group and headed toward him, thinking to intercept him as close to the door as possible. He appeared to be alone, on New Year's Eve, which seemed like an odd state for a newly engaged man.

"Hello, Savannah," he said when he drew near enough to be heard. "It's good to see you."

He reached for her hands, but she kept them at her sides. "Mitch. What are you doing here?"

"I saw your name on a gallery mailing about the spotlight, and decided to stop by and congratulate you."

"I would have thought you'd have other plans for New Year's Eve. With your fiancée."

A pained frown momentarily marred his handsome face. "She, uh…turned me down."

Ah. Now the reason for his presence became clearer. "Sorry to hear that. Don't worry. I'm sure the right girl will come along."

"I was thinking maybe she had, and I failed to recognize her. I mean, look at you. You've scored a showing with a premier gallery. I heard they're offering to represent you. You're back on track. I think we'd make a great couple—a successful lawyer and a successful artist. Unconventional, but in an interesting way."

Wow. The right connections and suddenly she'd been upgraded to marriage material. "I don't know, Mitch. I think I may still be too unconventional for you."

He took the statement as a challenge and smiled his confident lawyer smile. "Try me."

"I'm pregnant."

The smile disappeared. He paled and backed up a step. "That's impossible. You were on the pill, and we always used a condom."

Jeez. "It's not yours."

"Oh." For a moment she thought he might pass out from relief, but he pulled himself together. "Okay, well, then—" He trailed off awkwardly. "I guess you're involved with someone else."

"Guess again." Now she was just being mean, but some wicked part of her wanted to watch him squirm out of this hole he'd dug for himself with his version of a romantic, *When Harry Met Sally* New Year's Eve grand gesture. She stepped closer to him, crowding him a bit. "Still up for being part of an unconventional, yet interesting couple?"

"We should take some time to think this through. I mean, it's New Year's Eve, and we…I…got swept up in the excitement, but—"

"Relax, Mitch. I'm not interested. Nothing's changed for me. If anything, this baby cemented everything I always believed about love. I'm not after a relationship that makes sense on paper, or one that qualifies as unconventional, yet interesting. I want a soul mate, partner, and friend. I want a man who loves me for who I am, as I am. Who appreciates my strengths, and accepts my weaknesses…and…and…"

Oh my God.

She'd failed her own test. Beau had scars—weak points in his otherwise formidable strength. He'd shared them with her right from the start, and she'd claimed to understand, but when they got right down to it, she hadn't accepted him scars and all. She'd rejected his love as too damaged, and demanded he fix it. He'd asked her to stay, but she'd walked away because he hadn't been able to ignore his fears and paste a smile on his face. She needed to find him, talk to him, right now.

"I have to go," she mumbled, already in motion, fighting her way through the shifting kaleidoscope of shapes and colors to find the exit. She had it in view when the door opened and a man walked in.

Savannah skidded to a halt and let her greedy eyes feast on Beau for a moment while he scanned the room. For her?

He still wore his uniform, and stood out in rugged contrast to the polished suits and dresses surrounding him. He held something in his hands. People parted to let him through, all the while looking around to see who needed his attention.

Me. It's me. I need him.

But for some reason, her feet remained glued to the floor. She'd become performance art. *Woman Paralyzed with Regret.*

She knew the moment he saw her. His eyes locked onto her face, and her nerve endings tingled. Slowly, he approached. "I need a minute with you."

"I'm sorry," she stammered, and immediately started crying. Damn pregnancy hormones.

"No, I'm sorry. I know this isn't the right time or place. I'm the last guy you want to see, and I'm showing up like a selfish jerk and ruining your big night. Timing's not my strong suit, but I need to speak to you before you leave for Italy."

She had to talk around the lump in her throat. "I canceled the fellowship as soon as I learned I was pregnant. I didn't want to have my baby half a world away from home."

"Thank you," he said, and had the grace to look genuinely relieved. "Thank you for that, even if you had your own reasons for doing it."

She didn't know what to tell him about her reasons, so she stayed quiet.

"I want to introduce you to some people you should have met a long time ago." He held a book out to her. She took it and looked down to see a pink photo album. Her heart prepared to run, but she found her voice.

"Y-you don't have to…"

"I do." He flipped the book open, and a picture of a sweet,

tiny newborn in a little pink hat filled the page. Two deep, all-seeing eyes stared back at Savannah. Miniature versions of Beau's. "This is Abbey."

"She's beautiful."

"Yes," he agreed, and turned the page to a photo of a pretty, young brunette in a hospital bed, holding the baby and smiling a smile that radiated pride and adoration. "This is Kelli."

"Also beautiful," she managed, but the lump was back with a vengeance, and she couldn't say more.

He flipped through a few pages and opened the album to a picture of a younger Beau with one arm wrapped around his baby, and the other wrapped around his wife's shoulders. They stood in the shade of a big green maple tree. His smile reflected an unrestrained joy she hadn't seen from him since he'd been a little boy, chasing her around the swing set with his silly rubber snake.

"This was us."

Tears stung her eyes. He'd lost so much. Of course he feared losing again, and she'd been ruthless with his fear. "I'm so sorry."

"I was, too. I loved them. Having them in my life made me happier than I even realized until they were gone. And when they left, I would have done anything—bargained with the devil, sold my soul, traded my life—to have more time with them. Losing them hurt so much. The hurt faded after a while, but it will never completely leave."

"I understand. I do."

"The thing is, I've been so focused on the hurt I overlooked something important. I wouldn't trade a minute of my time with them. Not even to eliminate the pain. I'll always wish we'd had more time, but even knowing what I know now, I wouldn't have missed them for the world."

"I'm glad." She sniffed back tears and wiped her watering

eyes. "I know you loved them."

The lights went down around them. The crowd broke into a countdown.

Beau talked faster. "I did. They're an important part of my past. But you, and our baby? You're my future, and I don't want to miss this, either. I love you. I *want* to be there with you, and I want you with me—through every up and down. I'm all-in. No hedging. No holding back. I can handle anything except letting you walk out of my life. What do you say, Savannah? Will you take me on?"

She wrapped her arms around him and hung on. "Beau Montgomery, you have a hell of a way of wishing a girl happy New Year."

"It's my way of asking you to marry me. Take a risk on me, on us, and a happy new life."

"I'm all-in."

He kissed her as the lights strobed, and the crowd cheered, and people shouted, "Happy New Year!"

"Happy New Year to you, Smith," he whispered. Her knees went weak from the vibration of his voice in her ear and the sheer thrill of being pressed against him again, but to her surprise he suddenly drew away. She nearly swayed, but he dropped to his knees, clasped her waist in his big hands, and placed a gentle kiss on her stomach. "Happy New Year to you, little one."

"To us," she corrected when he stood and wrapped her in his embrace. "Happy New Year to us."

He kissed her again, long and slow, only raising his head when hers started to spin. He rested his forehead against hers, and she basked in the joy lighting his eyes.

"To us."

Acknowledgments

As always, I owe vital organs to a whole bunch of people for helping make Beau and Savannah's story a reality. Massive thanks to:

The whole awesome Entangled team, including Liz, Kari, Curtis, and Katie, but especially Heather, for sharing her ideas about a paramedic with a tragic past and a pie-baking artist—and believing I'd do them justice.

The insanely talented and generous Robin Bielman, for reading the first chapter and giving it a thumbs up, then holding her tongue when I re-wrote it, then not saying I-told-you-so when Heather told me the first version worked better.

The insanely talented and generous Hayson Manning, for reading the (more or less) final version and saying, (more or less), "Stop hacking at it, you paranoid fuck!"

The Romance Writers of America and the Los Angeles Romance Writers. I don't participate as often as I should, but in my mind, I am at every meeting and event, consuming the wisdom, guidance, and free food.

Charles and Hud, for being my real-life happily ever after.

My friends and family for encouragement and support that goes above and beyond the call of duty.

Readers, for being kind with praise, generous with subject-matter expertise (a/k/a smutty .gifs), and for trusting me with two very valuable things—time and money. Believe it or not, I try really hard not to be a waste of either.

About the Author

Wine lover, sleep fanatic, and USA Today Bestselling Author of sexy contemporary romance novels, Samanthe Beck lives in Malibu, California, with her long-suffering but extremely adorable husband and their turbo-son. Throw in a furry ninja named Kitty and Bebe the trash talking Chihuahua and you get the whole, chaotic picture.

When not dreaming up fun, fan-your-cheeks sexy ways to get her characters to happily-ever-after, she searches for the perfect cabernet to pair with Ambien.

BONDING GAMES

SECRET GAMES

BACHELOR GAMES

DIRTY GAMES

PROMISE ME

FAKING IT IN ALASKA

PLAYING DIRTY IN ALASKA

KNOCKED UP IN ALASKA

If you love sexy romance, one-click these Brazens…

HIS HOLIDAY CRUSH
a novel by Cari Z

One meeting away from making partner, Max Robertson is guilted into coming back home for Christmas. The plan is to go for just one night, but a wild deer and a snow bank wreck everything. Former Army Sergeant Dominic Bell of the Edgewood police has his evening turned upside-down when he gets called out to a crash—and it's his one and only high school crush. Everyone deserves a present this holiday season, right?

PLAYING WITH TROUBLE
a Sydney Smoke/Credence Crossover novel by Amy Andrews

Australian rugby pro Cole Hauser is ready for some peace and anonymity. The plan is perfect—until he discovers he's roomies with single mom Jane Spencer and her kid. While she's rehabbing the house in hopes it will put her business on the map, he's knee-deep in kid activities—and unexpectedly loving it. The situation is temporary, so it should be easy to say goodbye. However, it doesn't take long for them to realize they've borrowed a whole lot of trouble…but trouble never felt this good.

TAKING THE SCORE
a Tall, Dark, and Texan novel by Kate Meader

Paying down her sister's debts left personal assistant Emma Strickland with little more than the thrift store suit on her back and a second job as a waitress in a strip club. She'll do anything to keep her uptight, sexy-as-hell boss Brody Kane from finding out. But when he brings an important client to the club and gets the worst lap dance in adult entertainment history—from her—Brody makes it his mission to uncover her secrets, one illicit, over-the-desk encounter at a time.

Made in the USA
Las Vegas, NV
16 October 2023